I0761923

From *Hunt Mates*

The pricey flat-panel television atop the raised fork began to topple off.

Right over Emma's head.

Good packaging meant the TV would be fine. Her, not so much. Sure, her shifter nature could heal a few broken bones or concussion, but it would hurt like hell.

She danced aside, choosing not to test her shifter's healing.

Footfalls rang along the carpeted concrete from behind the forklift, getting nearer. "Damn it in milk, he's not supposed to be driving." Gabriel Light's voice, not the smooth baritone he'd used giving that speech, but deeper, hard and flat and determined.

"I'll fix it!" Brant jerked the steering wheel of the forklift. The box righted itself, wobbled...and started to fall the other way.

Right to where she'd moved.

An instant before she was smashed into a pulp by the plummeting television, strong arms scooped her from her feet.

A muscular leap carried her safe from disaster. Or at least the smaller, Brant-sized disaster. She'd barely comprehended that she wasn't hurt when she realized the full magnitude of the giant, Gabriel-Light-sized disaster.

Warm arms, thick with muscle and strong as tree trunks, plastered her to a chest as hard as polished contoured marble. Male scent filtered into her nose, crisp and clean and better than her best wet dream.

Her heart leaped and thudded. Slowly her eyes rose.

Gabriel Light's chiseled jaw was just a nibble away. Her tongue and teeth throbbed to take a taste.

"Brant, get off that thing." Dr. Light gazed sternly at the teen, a muscle ticking in his jaw. The man had insanely touchable-looking skin. "Ms. Singer, are you okay?"

She swallowed past her need, pushing away thoughts of insanely touchable skin. "I'm fine."

"Good. Sorry about that." Dr. Light's gaze was still on the forklift as he shook his head. "Brant the Blundering strikes again."

A laugh bubbled up in her throat. *Brant the Blundering?* "Appropriate."

"Yeah. I'd do something, but the kid desperately needs this job." His gaze shifted to Emma. Their eyes met.

Electricity leaped between them.

Her whole body went up in flames, as if a grain fire had whooshed inside her.

His pupils dilated abruptly and he swallowed hard. Gently, he set her on her feet.

She wobbled. His hands were instantly there, steadying her. She gazed into his eyes as if her soul was tethered to him.

"I have to...the missing phone..." He released her and dashed away.

Leaving her standing there, cold and shaken.

**"I loved the book!"** ~DebA, Night Owl Reviews on *Heart Mates* **TOP PICK**

**PUREST DELIGHT** "The way Mary Hughes finally brings her characters together—She has a way of having [Gabriel and Emma] **start off at a slow burn and then bring them together explosively**. It's always wild and fun." ~ Guilty Pleasures Book Reviews on *Mind Mates*

**"Non stop action and intense chemistry between Daniel and Zoe!** An exciting story which has me not so patiently waiting to find out what happens next." ~Jeanne M. on *Prophecy Mates*

"What a **brilliant, action packed, paranormal adventure and romance this proved to be**!" ~Splashes Into Books on *Mind Mates*

## Hunt Mates

*Her whole future is endangered by a theft. When her new boss finds out, will he condemn her or save her?*

Pull of the Moon Book 3

Iota wolf shifter Emma Singer has just snared a coveted job at Gabriel Light's Choice Buy store when a pricy high-tech phone is stolen—and it looks like Emma's the thief. How can she convince her new boss she's innocent?

Wizard prince Gabriel Light has bigger problems than the fact that his store has been robbed. A chance touch of his new hire lights a bonfire of lust in him. But witch + shifter = stupidly huge taboo. If the Witches' Council finds out, they'll have his head. Literally.

Yet the more Gabriel uncovers about the crime, the more unsettled he is. Especially when the thief returns and seems to be deliberately targeting Emma...

# Look for these titles by Mary Hughes

*Now Available:*

*Romantic Adventure*

Edie and the CEO—Crimson Romance

Falling ~~on~~ for the Billionaire

Cin Wikkid: April Fools For Love

Hot Chips and Sand

Bad Boy Billionaire's Lady: Lovless Brothers

Playing With Fire: The Battle of the Bands

*Biting Love/The Ancients*

Bite My Fire—Entangled

Biting Nixie—Entangled

The Bite of Silence—Entangled

Biting Me Softly—Entangled

Biting Oz—Entangled

Beauty Bites—Entangled

Downbeat—Entangled

Assassins Bite—Entangled

Passion Bites—Entangled

Biting Love Nibbles

Night's Caress—Entangled

*Pull of the Moon Series*
Prophecy Mates
Heart Mates
Hunt Mates
Mind Mates

*Standalone*
Black Diamond Jinn

*Coming Soon:*

The Classic Billionaire's Newshound (Lovless Brothers)
The Genius Billionaire's Hacker (Lovless Brothers)
Night's Kiss (The Ancients)
Night's Bliss (The Ancients)
Soul Mates (Pull of the Moon)

# Hunt Mates

## Pull of the Moon

Mary Hughes

Hunt Mates



Digital ISBN: 978-1-940958-19-4
Print ISBN: 978-1-940958-20-0
Editing by The Naughty Librarian's Playground
Cover by Scott Carpenter



First electronic publication: November 2017
First print publication: November 2017

# DEDICATION

To Gregg, as they all are.

Thank you to the Naughty Librarian for her gentle guidance editing and proofing. All mistakes are my own.

Waves to all my wonderful readers!

This story takes place after *Heart Mates* and prior to *Mind Mates*.

# Chapter One

Iota wolf shifter Emma Singer was a brand-new hire at the Muskegon Choice Buy store. She hadn't even met her new boss Dr. Light, when Brant tried to kill her for the first time.

"Can I help you, Emma?" Brant said brightly.

Emma paused squaring up boxes of phone accessories to consider the teenage boy. She and Brant were the only two trainees, wearing salmon-pink polo shirts instead of Choice-Buy blue.

He stood there beaming, a big industrial metal push broom in one too-big hand. *As eager as a puppy.*

All hands and feet, he was as coordinated as a puppy, too. She'd only been on the job a week, but she'd already cleaned up after him several times.

"Well..."

"Please?"

Emma heaved a sigh. The store manager, who'd been out of state when she was hired, returned tomorrow. Today needed all hands on deck getting the store spiffed up for his return.

"Okay." She gestured at a fallen headset blister pack. "Why don't you pick that up and find its proper place—"

"Thanks!" He scooped up the headset and rammed it onto an already full rod. The clip holding the rod to the display board broke loose. A dozen headsets tumbled onto the floor, one after the other like lemmings.

The boy's face fell. "Awww. I didn't mean to do that."

"I know you didn't." Emma shuffled through the mess of blister packs to pat the teen's arm gently.

"Ms. Singer!"

Shoulders tightening, Emma leaned out from behind Brant to see a sturdy blonde woman staring in horror at the mess.

Carol Palmer was the Assistant Manager. With silver hairs glinting among the blonde, in her Choice Buy blue polo shirt, she looked more like a professional golfer than a store manager. But she'd hired Emma, and had, in fact, put her professional reputation on the line for doing it. *"I shouldn't be hiring you, Emma. Dr. Light likes to screen all applicants himself. But he's away right now."*

"Dr. Light's coming back *tomorrow*." Carol briefly covered her eyes. "We don't have time for messes or mistakes."

"I'm so sorry, Ms. Palmer. I'll clean it up right away."

"Good." Heaving a stressed sigh, the woman squared her shoulders then trotted toward the next section of the store.

With a grimace, Emma picked up the rod, set it back into its clip, and hooked it to the display board. Fishing the nearest headset from the pile, she slid it carefully onto the rod.

"I can help!" Brant scooped up an armful of blister packs and hustled the heap toward the rod as if he'd shove them all on at once.

"Wait!" With a panicked yip, Emma barred him with her arm, half-shifted for strength. Her inner wolf was showing, but she was desperate to stop the boy, not only from another messy disaster, but from enthusiastically impaling himself on the rod.

He tottered back a step, his gaze bewildered.

"Why don't you let me reload the headsets?" She willed herself to move her arm away. "You can hold them for me if you want."

"That would help you?" Brant asked eagerly.

A twinge of sympathy hit her. The teen only wanted to be useful—just like her.

*We're only trying to please people...because nobody really wants us.*

She put a lid on the thought. "Yes," she told the boy firmly. "That will help me a lot."

Giving him an encouraging smile, Emma took a blister pack from the pile in his arms and threaded it onto the rod.

"So, Emma, do you think Dr. Light will give us our blue shirts when he comes back?"

"Make us real employees? We can hope." Emma, urgently needing work to provide for her widowed mother, had moved out of state to find a job. She'd been on the verge of accepting a menial, minimum wage position because it was available. Carol had offered her a six-month temp-to-hire contract with Choice Buy. Clean, well-run, good pay, plus her affinity for tech? Emma had snapped it up.

Loading the last blister pack onto its rod with great care, she considered what to do next. Face product—which she'd learned meant bring packages to the front of the shelf and lining them up without gaps—in the phone aisle? See if she could bang out a few laptop setups? She'd been trained on those.

But no, she'd probably better make sure Brant didn't get into any more trouble. "Thanks again, Brant. You really helped..." She looked up to see the teen's back disappearing around the corner of the display, the broom in one hand.

Curious and a little worried, she followed.

The shelves here were cut out, leaving an open area of floorspace. It was where the store displayed the big-ticket items.

Carol was fussing around the display table, extracting something from a Russian-stack-dolls' worth of boxes, tape, and packing peanuts. The Assistant Manager was fretting to herself. "Careful, Carol! Be careful."

Extracting a thin blade of plastic, the size and shape of a thick phone protector, she gently set it on the table.

Emma edged closer. Either that was one pricey phone shield, or it was something *new*.

"Why *today?*" Carol muttered a groan. "It wasn't supposed to arrive until Dr. Light got back." She glanced at Emma and must've realized she could hear her because her cheeks went ruddy. She spun and clapped her hands. "Gather up, people!"

Blue-shirted employees scuttled in, their curious eyes drawn immediately to the thin plastic rectangle resting on the display.

"Hush! This is important." Carol continued when they quieted, "This is a phone—with a five-thousand-dollar price tag."

Eyes all around her went wide.

"It's called the Wrapphone, made of bendable glass, this is the first commercially available wearable phone—potentially worth billions."

Emma's breath sucked in.

"We are stratospherically honored to be the site chosen to test market this phone. It even has a Holographic keyboard!" She plucked the thing off its stand and demonstrated, smoothing it into a cuff around her wrist then swiping until a keyboard made of light hovered just over her arm.

Gasps popped all around Emma. Eyes got even bigger and a few filled with tears.

"But you can still use it like a regular phone." Carol swiped back to deactivate the keyboard, pulled it off her wrist, and held it up to her ear to illustrate.

"Cool! Are all the Choice Buys selling it?" one employee asked.

"No. Nobody is because this is a prototype." She glared around the ring of blue-shirted employees. "*The only one in existence* until the company's manufacturing gets up to speed. They're seeing how many people might want to order it at this price point. We get to be the test market because Dr. Light has mega-connections. So if you screw this up..." Her gaze stopped to nail Brant.

He only beamed at her. But Emma shifted uncomfortably on her feet.

"*Nobody* touches this until you're trained. For now, any customer inquiries, come find me. Okay, now I'm going to lock this onto the display, and...damn." Carol hunted around the slanted plate that would hold the phone. Emma realized the curly steel security cable wasn't there. "I'm going to get the lock and be right back. No one touch this. Don't even breathe on it."

As Carol went to get the lock for the display, the rest of the employees dispersed.

Except for Brant, who stood with his industrial-sized metal broom, fingers flexing thoughtfully, staring at the empty boxes and packing peanuts that Carol had left on the floor. "Look at this mess. Ms. Palmer would want me to clean it up."

Emma put up a cautionary hand. "Maybe we should wait to ask Ms. Palmer..."

He'd already swirled into enthusiastic sweeping. Dust and packing peanuts went flying.

One especially exuberant spin hit the lowest shelf of phones. Models went flying.

Emma lunged toward the phones, hoping she could catch a few before they hit the thinly carpeted concrete floor—until she saw she had bigger problems.

The broom had jounced off the shelf, sailing straight into the air—on a direct collision course with the five-thousand-dollar Wrapphone.

Emma did the only thing she could. She twisted her body mid-lunge, trying to intercept Brant's broom.

At the same time Brant, his expression almost comically horrified, tried to avoid hitting her—by pulling the broom down.

The metal head, which should have hit her hands, whacked her in the skull.

Sharp pain exploded in her brain, her ears ringing a moment later with the aftershock. She landed in a stumble, nearly hitting the Wrapphone herself.

If she hadn't been a shifter, with unnaturally fast healing, she'd have had a concussion or worse. *He isn't* trying *to kill me,* she told herself. *Really.*

"Emma!" Brant dropped the broom and rushed her. "Are you all right?"

He tripped over his own big feet and blundered into her. She stumbled back into the table. The display holding the Wrapphone tottered.

*Or maybe he* is *trying to kill me.* If only by proxy, because if the phone fell and broke, Carol would wring Emma's neck.

Calling on her wolf, Emma grabbed the gangly teen in a tight hug then gave her whole body a prodigious twist. Their momentum sent them crashing into the rest of the phones on display. Plastic clattered and popped, along with a few teeth-shredding snaps.

Carol returned, jaw agape, lock cord dangling from her hand.

Emma smiled weakly at her. "Um, the Wrapphone's okay."

Carol's eyes clenched and Emma could almost see her teeth spark from grinding them so hard. Then older woman's lids opened, and she said in that honeyed tone all retailers learn to disguise their true feelings, "Brant, would you go back to the break room and...and count the napkins? Make sure we have enough?"

"Right away, Ms. Palmer!" Brant saluted—with the broom still in his hand. Emma threw up both forearms and barely saved herself a beaning. The impact smacked into her bones and vibrated down her skeleton.

"Hand me the broom, Brant. *Gently.*" Carol took the pole from him before he dashed away.

Emma hugged her arms to her. "I'm sorry about this, Ms. Palmer."

"No, it's my fault." The woman's gaze followed the boy as he disappeared. "But you need to remember—Dr. Light comes back tomorrow. He uses these cute breakfast-style swears, but make no mistake. Gabriel Light is as smart and strong as they come." Her gaze came to Emma, and caution sat there. "He'll make the final decision regarding your hire."

Emma swallowed hard. Carol was reminding her Gabriel Light liked to screen his own hires.

And if he saw anything like this...

"I'll be on my best behavior."

"Good."

# Chapter Two

Carding in the next day two seconds after seven a.m., Emma was extremely nervous. She'd wanted to make a good impression before—now she wanted to make a great one.

Today was the day. Today she'd meet Dr. Gabriel Light, store manager.

Today she'd find out if she still had a job.

She dropped her stuff off in her locker and immediately started work. "I'll be fine," she coached herself as she headed for the phone-accessories area, which always needed tidying. "Yes, he didn't actually hire me, but I'm pretty confident I'm getting the hang of things. Surely he'll give me a chance?"

She avoided the Wrapphone aisle. She definitely didn't want a replay of yesterday.

As she faced product on the shelves, she checked out the employees entering the store. She pictured Dr. Light as a counterpart to Carol, a solid man in his mid-forties or -fifties, maybe a pair of spectacles perched on his nose, as befitted the "Doctor".

Carol arrived a few minutes after Emma, immediately running around to check every area was neat and clean. As nervous or more so than Emma, which did not help Emma's nerves. As the blonde manager passed, she gave Emma a brief smile and thumbs up before running to check the next area. Emma swallowed her nerves and returned to straightening.

Every new person distracted her. More employees filtered into the store. Emma scanned their faces eagerly, looking for a middle-aged stranger with glasses. Most rang a vague bell from her first week on the job.

None of them looked like a Dr. Light to her.

Her head came up when a stranger glided in, black-haired and panther-like—but he didn't have glasses, so she went back to facing product. Finding a packaged headset out of place, she plucked it from the shelf and hunted for its proper spot. The blister pack reminded her of Brant yesterday. So touchingly eager. So clumsy. Brant Crandall had been here for almost six months, but he still wore trainee–salmon pink because the poor thing was more accident prone than a deer.

Awareness suddenly rippled through her belly.

She lifted her gaze. A bespectacled man had entered the store. *Dr. Light*?

But she'd expected a bent, middle-aged techie.

This man, striding confidently through the aisles, was head and shoulders above the shelves. Thick, dark hair, his shoulders broad and muscular.

She swallowed hard, her heart beating faster. Put his chiseled profile on a rockstar, and panties would be wet enough to drench the Sahara. Hers were certainly sliding.

This Dr. Light was taller and younger and stronger than she'd pictured. And much, much, sexier.

Then he prowled into the open.

She'd expected the unfashionable, shapeless clothes, a slouchy sweater vest over the Choice Buy polo and baggy slacks.

But the way he moved, that was no shapeless body beneath.

No, his prowl was all muscular elegance, as if the man's strength and power was so elemental it couldn't be disguised by something so ordinary as cloth.

Emma's body went haywire. She dropped the headset.

The clack of plastic hitting the floor drew her attention, but she was so flabbergasted at the sight of Dr. Light, she only blinked down at the package at her feet. Something about that was wrong. She needed to...needed to do something.

Her job. Product on shelf. Wow. Something about that achingly tall, lickably muscular, reeking of power...that *man* had really done a number on her. She bent and picked up the headset with trembling fingers. Still half-bent, she hunted for the package's proper place among all the others on the shelf. A task that had been routine and easy had become impossibly hard, as if her brain someplace far, far away.

*Locked onto a warrior's muscular prowl and a prince's noble profile.*

Her body froze, her eyelids blinking rapidly. Where had that thought come from?

The man passed her on his way to the home entertainment area. Her wolf caught his scent.

Her whole body went on the fritz.

Every nerve, organ, and cell lit up as if she'd been plugged into a wall socket...*or as if he's my mate.*

Shocked, she snapped straight. Couldn't be. Wolf mated wolf, and Gabriel Light smelled all-too-human, though deliciously masculine.

He walked away from her, revealing powerful shoulder blades and narrow hips. Her pelvis ached with need, her thighs desperate to wrap around those hips, and she had a sudden desire to find out if he was as well-muscled as she thought—by stripping those slouchy clothes from his big body with her teeth.

She clenched her jaw against a silent groan. *Human.* Shifters, even of iota caliber, were unusually strong and highly sexed. He'd never keep up.

*He's big, though. That size? He might be able to handle me and my iota.*

Her inner wolf began wagging its tail. She took an involuntary step after him, her mind already catapulting to what she'd say, what he'd say.

*"Hi, sexy. Come here often?"*

*"Hi. Are you the woman I had no say in hiring?"*

She stopped cold. *Barking* idiot. *I need this job.* If that was Dr. Gabriel Light, and she was pretty sure he was, he was her boss. At best he'd think any proposition from her as forward, and at worst, he'd think she was trying to sleep her way into a permanent position.

The rest of the employees were gathering around the home theater section. Emma wedged the headset into the first available space and joined them around a raised platform.

The big man mounted the platform, a mega-screen television behind him haloing his thick head of hair. As she neared, she realized the man wasn't just big, he was a giant, around six and a half feet.

"For those of you who don't know me, I'm Gabriel Light, store manager. Let me say how great it is being back. It takes seeing the mess of another family to make you appreciate your own." He launched into a short speech, the other employees listening attentively.

The closer she got, the more gorgeous he was to her. Perfect jaw, chiseled lips, strong nose. Her stomach shimmied.

"I've always thought my people were the best..." His head turned—straight toward Emma.

His gaze locked with hers. His eyes consumed her, deep blue-green irises shot with startling silver. Those star-shot gaze zinged straight into her sex. She throttled a groan.

He cleared his throat and switched his gaze to the person beside her. "I've always thought you are the best of the best, but now I know it."

Without his gaze tethering her, her brain began working again. Had he paused? She frowned. Strange, when he was so fluent before. But she wasn't really sure because she'd been so discombobulated by his amazing eyes.

"I'll finish by welcoming our new hire. Now, let's go have fun!"

*Welcome the new hire...? That's* me. Emma got a glow of belonging, quickly suppressed. He was just being diplomatic. He wouldn't want to undermine Carol's hire in front of the rest of the employees. He might still fire Emma in private.

But it still felt so nice to be included.

The meeting broke up. Emma stood there, torn. She wanted to meet Gabriel Light with an urgency that shook her. But if he saw how attracted she was, that might be the first step to job suicide.

*Might not,* her inner wolf yipped.

*Mom needs the money I earn,* she scolded herself. *Now's not the time to indulge in fantasy.*

The stream of people heading back to work pulled her with them. She needed this job, and she wouldn't have it much longer standing there, mooning over her boss.

Forcing herself to move, she turned away from Dr. Light's commanding presence.

Only to see a panicked Carol running back toward them.

"The wrap-phone prototype is gone. It's been stolen!"

# Chapter Three

Shock iced Emma's lungs. The Wrapphone was gone? While she'd been facing stock one aisle over?

Had a thief taken it under her nose?

*Puh-lease,* her inner wolf sniffed. She stifled a laugh. Under a wolf's nose? No way. She'd have smelled something off.

"Keep calm, everyone," Dr. Light said.

Glancing over her shoulder, she saw him stride purposefully off the platform, headed toward Carol. Emma scooted out of his path, along with a handful of other employees.

"I'll look into it and if necessary, call the police. In the meantime, that shipment of new plasma screens has come in. I'd love to see them on the shelf before the store opens. Carol, could you see to it?"

"Yes, sir." The assistant manager nodded, panic leaving her body and suddenly all business. "David, Joy, and Emma, please clear the way for the forklifts. Ann, Joe, and Brant, come with me."

Emma was frankly admiring. He'd calmed all their panic and then put everyone into a productive mode with just a few deft actions.

She'd already memorized the routes the forklifts used to bring product onto the floor. Starting at the doorway to the loading dock, she began sliding displays from the path to the home theater area.

Minutes later, a forklift came roaring out of the back, a six-foot television carton atop the forks, careering near-misses with the heavily stocked shelves. Emma straightened with a sucked-in breath.

At the wheel of the forklift was the gangly teen Brant.

The vehicle swerved. A set of high-end cameras was on its way to being so much shrapnel.

Emma didn't think, she just acted, dashing out, waving and calling. "Brant! This way." Her arms scissored like an Airforce signal officer or a demented puppet, trying to guide him in. When he headed for her, she leaped to shove clear the last few displays before he hit them. "Okay stop. Stop!"

Half a foot from her, he squealed to a halt.

She released a relieved breath—too soon.

The pricey flat panel atop the raised fork began to topple off.

Right over her head.

Good packaging meant the TV would be fine. Her, not so much. Sure, her shifter nature could heal a few broken bones or concussion, but it would hurt like hell.

She danced aside, choosing not to test her shifter's healing.

Footfalls rang along the carpeted concrete from behind the forklift, getting nearer. "Damn it in milk, he's not supposed to be driving." Gabriel Light's voice, not the smooth baritone he'd used giving that speech, but deeper, hard and flat and determined.

"I'll fix it!" Brant jerked the steering wheel of the forklift. The box righted itself, wobbled...and started to fall the other way.

Right to where she'd moved.

An instant before she was smashed into a pulp by the plummeting television, strong arms scooped her from her feet.

A muscular leap carried her safe from disaster. Or at least the smaller, Brant-sized disaster. She'd barely comprehended that she wasn't hurt when she realized the full magnitude of the giant, Gabriel-Light-sized disaster.

Warm arms, thick with muscle and strong as tree trunks, plastered her to a chest as hard as polished contoured marble. Male scent filtered into her nose, crisp and clean and better than her best wet dream.

Her heart leaped and thudded. Slowly her eyes rose.

Gabriel Light's chiseled jaw was just a nibble away. Her tongue and teeth throbbed to take a taste.

"Brant, get off that thing." Dr. Light gazed sternly at the teen, a muscle ticking in his jaw. The man had insanely touchable-looking skin. "Ms. Singer, are you okay?"

She swallowed past her need, pushing away thoughts of insanely touchable skin. "I'm fine."

"Good. Sorry about that." Dr. Light's gaze was still on the forklift as he shook his head. "Brant the Blundering strikes again."

A laugh bubbled up in her throat. *Brant the Blundering?* "Appropriate."

"Yeah. I'd do something, but the kid desperately needs this job." His gaze shifted to Emma. Their eyes met.

Electricity leaped between them.

Her whole body went up in flames, as if a grain fire had whooshed inside her.

His pupils dilated abruptly and he swallowed hard. Gently, he set her on her feet.

She wobbled. His hands were instantly there, steadying her. She gazed into his eyes as if her soul was tethered to him.

"I have to...the missing phone..." He released her and dashed away.

Leaving her standing there, cold and shaken.

* * *

Wizard Prince Gabriel Light got the hell out of scent range of the pretty little she-wolf before she got a whiff of him.

Before she could scent the testosterone pouring off him like Niagara Falls.

Holding her warm, curvy little body, smelling her sweet, wild scent...he'd ignited in a bonfire of lust. He could smell it.

And if he could, she certainly could.

He strode from the store proper into the back area, making straight for his office. There, he locked himself in and activated the wards.

Throwing himself into his chair, he dragged exasperated hands through his hair. *Scrambled eggs and damn. What do I do now?*

While he was out of state last week, Carol had texted him about the new hire, and on paper he agreed with her scooping Ms. Singer up. He'd been prepared to ratify his assistant's decision this morning as soon as he'd seen the small woman working so industriously. He went toward her to introduce himself, opening his third eye on her just as a matter of routine—and had been astonished to see her pulse with magic.

*A shifter.*

That changed things. Shifters didn't care much for witches. True, she wouldn't know he was a witch, as magic was only visible in a thing or being of magic, like a talisman or shifter. Witches, as manipulators of magic, weren't visible to the third eye.

He didn't intend to mislead her, but he couldn't have mundane ears overhearing him when he told her. Regular people didn't, *couldn't* know about magic. Magic was all about manipulating the power of possibility. If everyone knew it was real, magical possibility would become concrete and collapse into mundane reality. Poof, no more magic.

So he'd decided to tell Ms. Singer in private, and had passed her to give his glad-to-be-home speech, meaning to call her into his office later.

Then Carol had shouted that the Wrapphone was missing. He'd called the police and had been busy searching the area when Brant caromed out on that forklift.

Gabriel was rarely rash. He kept a belt of talismans for just about every eventuality, from calm spells for pissed-off customers to a find spell for lost children. He'd reached under his vest for a discreet Slow when he'd seen Ms. Singer in imminent danger.

Something primitive inside him went from zero to sixty in two seconds flat. He'd abandoned spells to dive in personally, leaping to her rescue like he'd grown tights and a cape.

The instant he felt her curvy warm body and smelled her soft femininity and fell into her big brown eyes he started spurting testosterone like a gorilla. But, holy cereal bombs, the new hire was the most beautiful morsel of a woman he'd ever seen...and as he stood there, wanting her with every fiber of his being, he realized he was a crunchy-in-milk *idiot.*

Witch. Shifter. Huge taboo.

If the Witches' Council, the magical community's governing body, found out he was insanely attracted to a shifter, they'd have his head.

Literally.

Ever since an insane werewitch king had tried to take over the world, witch/shifter sex was declared illegal, immoral, and fattening—as in, *we'll remove ten pounds instantly, not with liposuction but with an axe.*

For himself, he might have risked the headsman's axe to try for a coffee date, or for dinner and a movie followed by a little meaningless sex... His groin wrenched with need. He dug his hands deeper into his hair, pulling the roots, hoping a little scalp pain might keep him from dashing right back out there for more caveman rescuing.

He forced himself to remember it wasn't just his life on the line. Ms. Singer would also get penalized, and the Council's Enforcers usually hit the female with the worst of the punishment.

He couldn't stand the idea of one hair on Emma's head being harmed.

*Emma?*

*I mean Ms. Singer.*

He'd have to tell Ms. Singer everything. If she wasn't attracted in return, problem solved. If she was...well, maybe between the two of them, they could figure out a way to deal with it.

Except she might not care what the Council thought. Shifters often didn't. And she was a wolf, highly sexed. She might not only not say no to a coffee date followed by a little meaningless sex, she might throw him to the floor, throw one leg over his hips and...

He clenched his eyes. His groin was on fire simply from imagining she'd want him. Much more of this and he'd be coming in his pants. Imagine if she actually told him she desired him, too?

Then how could he keep her safe? He found himself filled with a fiery need to do just that.

Change of plans. *Don't tell her any of it. Don't tell her I'm a witch, don't tell her I want her so badly I'd risk the headsman's axe just to steal a kiss.*

*And especially don't let her smell the desire wafting off me.*

Resolutely he stood and reached under his sweater vest for his belt of ready talismans—he wasn't just a wizard prince, he was a battle mage and always kept his belt stocked.

It took a lot of raw power to throw a spell, which was why most witches prepared talismans in advance. Like a battery versus plugging in, talismans were easy and quick but limited, whereas a witch's personal well of power, while easily depleted, eventually recharged.

His office was innocent-looking enough, his desk, his executive chair, two guest chairs, a set of filing cabinets, and a supply cabinet. A credenza lined most of one wall, the area over it tiled with beaming photographs of all his employees.

But underneath the ordinary was the magical, just waiting to be revealed.

Finding the talisman he wanted, he touched it, releasing its prepared spell. The air above the credenza shimmered, revealing his cauldron and other spell-casting paraphernalia sitting atop.

He couldn't let Emma—*Ms. Singer*—smell his desire, therefore he had to magic a way to keep the stink hidden.

Considering his options, he took down several talisman blanks and got to work.

# Chapter Four

Choice Buy's doors opened to the public at nine. Emma wasn't trained in customer service yet, so she retreated to the public workbench near the checkouts, which they called the Techie Titan Base. The horseshoe of neatly stacked equipment and paperwork was cut in half by a freestanding wall, the front half public, the back half private.

She lifted the gate to enter Base, grabbed the top couple work orders in the stack, and retreated behind the wall to begin setting up the first laptop.

As Emma worked, she chewed over Dr. Light's rescuing her. And hadn't his heroic save made her belly swoop delightedly? But then he'd retreated like she'd suddenly sprouted boils. She was at a loss as to why. What had happened? Had he seen the desire in her eyes and been uncomfortable, or worse offended?

But she'd sniffed the barest dusting of testosterone in the air.

If he'd been offended, surely she wouldn't have caught that trace of desire.

Well, in the final analysis, it didn't matter why he'd retreated, only that he *had* retreated. If he hadn't, she might have considered asking him out for coffee, or a date, or a little hot man-on-shifter action... She clenched her eyes briefly. He was her boss and she needed this job. Let him make the first move if there was a move to be made. She'd just have to ignore her attraction in the meantime.

Work like hell to earn his respect.

She'd just resolved this when a voice said from the other side.

"Hello, ma'am. I'm Your Name. I mean, I'm Brant. How can I help you today?"

Emma popped to her feet. What was the saying—bad things come in threes? After the broom incident yesterday and the television incident today, this was a disaster in the making.

She came around to see Brant grinning at a red-faced customer holding a laptop without a case.

"This piece of junk doesn't work. Your store sold me this crap, and I want my money back." She slapped it down on the counter.

"Um..." Brant stared down at an open binder on the desk just below the lip of the counter. Emma sidled closer until she could just see the top of the page, where "Hello sir/ma'am. I'm Your Name. How can I help you?" was printed.

Emma figured it must be a decision tree manual.

Brant started flipping pages in the manual. Each page was labeled with a large cause, like Problem With Billing, Problem With Finding an Item. He stopped at Problem with Computer.

The first paragraph read, "Have you tried turning it off and back on?"

Brant raised his gaze to the customer with a grin, ill-advised from the blood coloring her face and the vein pulsing in her forehead. “Have you tried turning it off and back on?”

“Yes,” the woman ground out. “Several times. It won’t turn on at all! It’s a defective piece of crap even a toilet would reject.”

“Um, okay.” Brant threw a “help me” glance toward Emma.

She wasn’t trained in customer service, but she couldn’t leave the poor boy helpless. “Hello, ma’am. I’m Emma, and we’ll do everything we can to get your problem resolved. If you’ll just let me find a senior Techie Titan—”

“Look at it! It’s so obviously defective even I can see it.” The customer grabbed the laptop and flipped it over. “It’s got this huge hole in it!”

Emma stared. It did have a hole in it—because the battery was missing.

“Oh.” A totally inappropriate laugh rose in Emma’s throat. She kept it down, but she could feel her face get red. “Well, um...I’ll just go get someone to help you.” She raised the gate and spun out—only to nearly run into an impressive chest covered by yards of sweater vest.

Gabriel Light.

He’d heard the whole exchange.

Emma wanted to melt into a puddle of embarrassment. So much for impressing him. “Oh, Dr. Light. I’m glad you’re here. This customer needs some laptop help.” She raised her gaze.

“I see.” His blue-green eyes twinkled behind his glasses. Laughing at her—or *with* her? He turned to the customer with graceful aplomb. “Ma’am, I’m Gabriel Light. We’re here to help.”

Nothing Emma and Brant hadn't done, but coming from Dr. Light, the phrases seemed almost magical. The customer's red face ebbed and, for the first time, she smiled.

"What Brant and Emma were about to say is that you need a battery to power your laptop. Mr. Crandall, check in the back for part number..." He named a series of letters and numbers. Seeing Brant just standing there, Emma quick reached over the counter, grabbed pencil and paper, and jotted the part number down.

When she raised her gaze, Dr. Light was smiling at her. "Ms. Singer, if you could help him?"

"Yes, sir."

"Thank you."

Just then Carol swept up. "Dr. Light, the man from the insurance company is here."

"Ah, the claims adjuster. That was quick. Please take him to my office, and I'll meet him as soon as I'm done here."

* * *

After getting the battery and seeing off a now-satisfied customer, Emma ducked back behind the wall separating the public and private section of Base.

Several hours later, she was quietly working when she heard a voice.

"I'm worried, Pan," Carol said from the other side of the wall. "I don't know what happened. The Wrapphone was here last night when I went home. Maybe it just got moved?"

"Dr. Light and I searched the whole store. It's definitely gone."

The bass voice was roughened by a growl. It reminded Emma of the tall, black-haired man whose panther's grace had been interesting—until Dr. Light's entrance had wiped it, and everything else, from her mind.

"And you saw the detective," the man called Pan continued. "He's treating it like a crime scene."

"He didn't say it was stolen."

"He won't give anything away until he's come to his conclusions."

"Maybe. But he keeps glaring at *me*. Like he suspects me. It makes me nervous."

"Don't worry. If he accuses you, Dr. Light'll set him straight."

A brief silence. Then, sounding tentative, Carol said, "What did you think of the insurance adjuster?"

"Dickwad," Pan growled.

Carol laughed, but it sounded a little nervous. "He seems to think one of us took the phone."

Emma's hands froze on the keyboard.

"Yeah, well, it makes unfortunate sense," Pan said. "The building is locked after hours, and there's no indication of a break-in."

"But an employee theft? It's ridiculous. None of the staff that's been here for any time at all would do that to Dr. Light."

"They all know not to cross him," Pan said.

"Or you." Carol's voice held a shudder. "There's a reason you're first assistant manager. Your chewings-out are legendary." Another silence, extremely uncomfortable for Emma. "But if not one of the permanent staff, then..."

"Yeah," Pan growled. "It has to be one of the new hires."

All the feeling left Emma's limbs. Her hands dropped to either side of the keyboard, suddenly too heavy to move.

Tentatively, Carol said, “Brant?”

“The kid?” Pan snorted. “He’s not smart enough. Even if he managed to unlock the Wrapphone from the display, he’d be standing out in the middle of the store with the thing.”

“But that leaves...”

Carol left the name unsaid, but Emma knew the answer.

That left her.

Oh, why had *this* store been the test market? If the phone had already been a commodity item, several billion sold, instead of one of a kind, she wouldn’t be in danger of worse than losing her job.

Being declared a criminal. She shuddered.

And then her phone buzzed. Premonition making her heart sink, she took it out.

New text.

*—Pls come to my office. GL—*

# Chapter Five

Emma stood in front of Dr. Light's closed office door, nerving herself to knock. Less than two weeks ago, when she interviewed with Carol Palmer, this door had stood open, a doorway representing a new opportunity.

Now she was suspected of a crime and the door was closed. She feared the symbolism was all too plain.

She raised her fist. Before she could knock, the door suddenly flew open to a broad, heaving chest barely confined by its polo and sweater vest.

Her startled gaze flew up...and up. At over a foot taller than her, standing so very close, Gabriel Light was a big man indeed. From his white nostrils and narrow eyes behind his glasses, the big man was also an angry man.

Angry he'd gone to so much trouble to get that phone here, only to have it stolen?

Probably angriest at her, as the most likely thief.

"Ms. Singer. Please come in." His tone, in contrast to his tense frame, was polite. So he was angry, but controlling it well. Already he was a step above most of the wolves in her pack. He moved back, waving her inside.

She cleared her throat as she crossed the threshold. “Please, call me Emma.”

“Emma.” One corner of his mouth quirked, as if that made him smile despite his anger. Then the grim line of his lips was back. “This is Mr. Omniss.” He stabbed a hand in the direction of a fussy little man perched in the big chair behind the desk. “He’s with the company insuring the Wrapphone.”

Or maybe her boss’s rage was directed at the insurance adjuster who was in Dr. Light’s chair, lording it over his office. She knew alpha wolves who would have ripped off Omniss’s head for such an affront.

“Emma Singer.” The man didn’t even bother looking at her. He ticked a box on the sheet of paper before him with an accusatory scratch. “You just started last week. How convenient.” Now he did flick up a pointed glance to match the sneer in his words. “Sit.” He pointed his pen at the guest seat, which was squared with the big desk like an electric chair.

She quailed.

“Please sit, Emma.” Dr. Light sliced Omniss a rebuking glare then gently pulled the chair out for her, turning it slightly away from the adjuster, as if trying to spare her having to confront the man directly. As she eased onto the cushion, he touched her shoulder reassuringly. “Don’t worry. We’re simply interviewing all the employees to see if they remember anything.”

She perched on the chair with a grateful smile, relaxing. He smiled gently back.

Then he spoiled it by starting to pace. He was really worried. She knotted her hands in her lap. Burped in her nervousness. A smell like rancid beef hit her.

Darn. She knew she shouldn't have had that leftover burger for breakfast.

"I bet you remember something, Emma." Omniss bared teeth at her, leaning threateningly toward her. "I bet you remember *everything*."

The aggressive question threw her. Any rancid beef scent flew from her head. "I-I don't know what you mean—"

"Omniss, watch your tone." Dr. Light stopped abruptly, arms crossed over his chest, and hit the insurance man with such a narrow stare, Emma was surprised Omniss didn't bleed. "That's my employee you're talking to."

"That's *my* prime suspect."

Emma's heart leaped into her throat. "I didn't take the phone."

"So you say. But you have an employee keyfob, don't you? You had access—that's means and opportunity, two of the detective's golden trinity. And Carol mentioned you made no secret of needing this job, which means you're strapped for cash." His eyes glittered, small and mean and triumphant. "So you had motive—"

"That's *enough*." A single long-legged step brought Dr. Light to stand beside her. Wedging himself as a shield between her and Omniss, he leaned knuckles on the desk and scowled at the adjuster.

His narrow eyes were joined by a clenched jaw, white knuckles, and a low, thrumming growl, signaling such clear and present danger that Emma's iota wolf tucked tail. Even Omniss flinched.

Barely heard through his clenched jaw, Dr. Light ripped out, "You will treat my employees with respect or you will leave. Am I clear?"

"Clear," the adjuster whispered.

"Good."

The moment stretched, as if Dr. Light was barely keeping himself from tearing the man limb from limb.

Emma cleared her throat tentatively. "The phone was secure in its display yesterday. I didn't look at it this morning, but I was working one aisle over from a little after seven until Dr. Light made his speech, and I didn't smel..." She caught herself barely in time. Smelling the thief wouldn't make sense to mundanes. "I didn't see or hear anyone."

Dr. Light released his clenched jaw, lifted his fists from the desk, and stepped back. But he didn't release the fists as he folded his arms over his chest, for once not bothering to hide his height or strong, muscled body. "I gave a short address half an hour before the doors opened at nine."

The insurance adjuster glanced at him, then met her gaze. "So you'd have us believe the thief struck either before seven this morning or after eight thirty." His rolled his eyes.

"Yes, sir. I'd have at least heard him or her snap the cable." Emma said.

"The cable wasn't broken," the man said sharply.

Emma's cheeks heated. She hadn't considered that there might be more evidence than the timing pointing to an employee. But then she realized, "Unlocked? But that proves it wasn't me. I'm a trainee. I don't have a security unlocker—"

"You have access to them, don't you?"

There was one in every sales station drawer or cabinet. "All employees do," she mumbled. She wanted to sink into the chair and disappear.

"We're done here." Dr. Light strode to the door and threw it open. "Thank you for coming, Emma. Could you send Brant in next?"

"Yes, sir." She got unsteadily to her feet. "I'll go get him." She managed to stumble to the door.

As she passed him, he bent and asked softly, "Are you okay?"

* * *

*Are you okay?*

*No. And I haven't been for a long, long time.*

At one time Emma had been better than okay. She'd been the beloved daughter of a doting father. Sure, she had an older brother who called her "Mouseturd" and a mother who mostly ignored her, and her parents ritual mating meant they weren't soul mates. But Emma's father was a favored lieutenant in the pack, and as status meant everything to Emma's mother, they were reasonably happy.

Then Dickie Bloodfang killed their alpha, took over their pack, and ritually slaughtered all the old alpha's lieutenants. Including Emma's father.

Leaving Emma's family lowest of the low. Vulnerable.

Emma's mother tried to raise their status by bedding Dickie's brother. Emma, misunderstanding, interfered spectacularly, nearly killing Dickie's brother. Emma's mother immediately moved the family out of state, to her birth-pack.

But ever after, Emma was treated differently. She'd already been her mom's least-favored child of the family. Now she was barely tolerated. Living in a strange town, running with a strange pack, didn't help her sense of alienation.

She learned to say "I'm fine" because nobody cared if she wasn't. She learned to always be helpful because that was the only time she wasn't hated.

She learned to win approval through actions. It wasn't love, but it was the next best thing—and the only way she ever felt wanted.

* * *

*Are you okay?*

"I'm fine." The words came out automatically. She was anything but fine.

Dr. Light hesitated. "All right. Send Brant."

As she left, he closed the door firmly behind her. She felt it like a hit between her shoulder blades.

Carol met Emma coming out of the office. The assistant manager's eyes were wide and sparkling.

"Wow. You must've really pissed that prissy little man off."

Emma's shoulders hunched. "I didn't mean to. But he thought I was the thief—without any proof. How did you know?"

"I heard Dr. Light all the way in the break room. That was his 'Nobody messes with my employees' voice." Carol smiled.

*His employees*. It made Emma feel slightly better. Sure, she wasn't loved, but as one of Gabriel Light's employees, he'd protect her. After the spectacular mess she'd made of her family, she felt that was better than she deserved.

Emma tagged Brant, making sure the teen was on his way to the back office before she returned to the Techie Titan Base. She picked up the computer setup order she'd been working on, but after a few half-hearted pokes, she leaned back with a sigh. The insurance adjuster unfortunately had a point. Means, motive, and opportunity shone a spotlight squarely on her.

So she was under suspicion—prime suspect, really. She desperately didn't want to go to prison, or lose this job. Strangely, almost as important, she didn't want to disappoint Dr. Light.

She knew she wasn't the thief, but the insurance investigator was convinced it was her, and he might convince everyone else. What could she do?

Well, it was obvious. Find the thief herself.

Her whole being perked up at the thought. She could clear her name by doing her own investigation. Resolutely, she pushed the laptop away and got to her feet.

The more she thought about it, the better she liked it. She had the advantage over the police and the insurance adjuster because she knew she was innocent. Heck, she'd probably do a better job because she could use her wolf.

She trotted to the area where the Wrapphone had been on display, in the prominent cutout area at the head of a double-wide aisle.

The display table was fenced off by four posts joined by yellow crime scene tape. A crew of men and women in paper booties and hoods swarmed the area with measuring tapes and fingerprint brushes and cameras.

She hesitated. Investigating now would attract unwanted attention.

She'd have to wait until after they'd gone.

Actually, if she wanted to make sure she was undisturbed and could use her full wolf senses, she'd have to wait until after the store was closed and all the employees were gone.

Okay, but wouldn't hiding out look suspicious?

Then she remembered the Wrapphone had already been stolen and she was the prime suspect. How could she get in hotter water than that?

She returned to Base and finished setting up the computer, chafing inside as she waited for closing. After working her shift, she went out to pick up some dinner. The Choice Buy was in a strip-mall park, and there were plenty of options, from a burger joint to a sandwich shop to her favorite coffee bar. Tonight she grabbed a quick cheeseburger, returning with her supper to the Choice Buy employee lunch room. She ate her burger and slurped her chocolate shake, pretending to read an ebook but really she was just chafing some more.

As the last customer left, she went to hide in the ladies' room. While Carol did her final sweep, Emma sat on the tank in the restroom, feeling foolish and excited and anxious and determined, until the assistant manager clicked onto the store intercom with the all-call. "Anyone still in the building, please let me know..." Emma counted slowly to sixty five times, to give the assistant manager time to set the store alarm. Then she crept out of the stall and into the store proper, worried momentarily that she'd trip some internal alarm.

All was still.

A little more confident but still ultra alert, she trotted toward the main phone display area.

Though the police investigators had finished dusting for prints and taking photographs long ago, she still smelled powder in the air. And the tape was still up.

*Crime Scene—Do Not Cross.*

She hesitated. Suddenly she realized if she went into the cordoned-off square, she'd look like she was returning to the scene of the crime to gloat—or get rid of evidence.

No, all the evidence had already been collected. Besides, she had to get closer if she wanted to sort out the different scents.

Right. Doing this.

Ducking under the tape, she took in the table display. Everything looked normal except for the empty phone stand. Sure enough, the anti-theft cable dangled, uncut, pointing very firmly to an inside job.

Time to use her wolf nose to scent the area. She took a delicate sniff. Traces of scent intrigued her, none strong enough to identify, although she caught the edges of what might have been adolescent male, and a touch of a rancid beef scent, although that could have been her dinner.

*I need more information.*

She sucked in a deep breath—got a noseful of fingerprint powder and sneezed.

A deep voice came from behind her.

"Bless you."

# Chapter Six

Heart leaping into her throat, Emma jerked around.

Her big boss stood there on the other side of the tape, a slight smile on his handsome face.

"Oh! Dr. Light. I was just...I, er..." Her brain fogged with an odd combination of embarrassment and excitement. Her tongue felt like it belonged to someone else. Her wolf was happily wagging its tail.

"Investigating? Me too." He lifted one leg and stepped easily over the tape barrier. "I don't trust that Omniss to get it right."

She blinked at him. Besides the casual display of leg strength that made her wolf wag its tail harder, he'd not only understood what she was doing, not only approved, he was *doing it too?*

An image of him and her, *doing it too,* painted her brain in colors of bow-chicka-wow-wow. She clenched her eyes.

"And it's after hours, Emma. You don't have to call me Dr. Light. Yes, I like a little formality at work—it creates a space so if I have to take disciplinary action, employees don't feel like a friend is punishing them—but it's okay to call me Gabriel now."

"Oh, well, um..." She opened her eyes and tried to give him a bright, non-sexual smile. "I would, but I'm still a trainee and it doesn't feel right. And what if it gets to be a habit and I forget during the day? Maybe I'd better not."

He considered her for long moments, and she worried he'd take offense. But then he simply smiled. "Okay. What have you discovered?"

She released a relieved breath. "Nothing much. I just got started." She turned from all that was male and glorious and tried to get a better scent of the thief, disguising her actions with an intent stare at the empty stand. Everything was overlaid by the scent of the crime scene techs, but fortunately theirs were fainter because of their coveralls. She sifted through the smells for the strange male. *There*. She caught it again. Definitely a man, with a heavy tang of testosterone. So either aroused—by stealing, *eww*—or he was young and still producing lots of the stuff. She ignored the scent of meat to sort through the layers, identifying a curl of cologne woven into the male's scent. Without knowing what kind of cologne, she'd guess the vanity of youth. The combination made it more likely the man was young.

"What do you see?" Her boss's deep voice came softly from behind her. As he stepped to her side, his breath touched her cheek.

Minty, fresh. Perfect for drinking in through a deep kiss with lots of tongue... She suppressed a shiver of lust, covering it with a bright smile at him. "Well...if I had to guess, the thief is a young male."

"Why is that?" He cocked a questioning brow above his glasses.

She felt her face heat. Why? Because she smelled it. But she couldn't tell him that. Time to distract him with random facts. "As Omniss said, the antitheft cable is still intact. The phone holster doesn't look broken." She pulled a pen from her pocket and tipped the holster to see it better. "And the alarm box is still intact, too. The siren would have gone off if the lock wasn't properly opened. So it's likely the key was used."

"Good theory." Dr. Light's tone was approving. She stood a little straighter. He continued, "Sorry about Omniss grilling you earlier. You were the first one called in. I had no idea he was going to be such a prick."

That surprised a laugh from her. It was funny hearing her boss, dressed in all his college-professor glory, saying "prick".

"Thanks for intervening. Is he an adjuster or an investigator?"

He made a face. "His title is adjuster. But the way he's treating us, I think he *thinks* he's the investigator, judge, and executioner all in one."

His use of "us" heartened her even more.

"There is one other way to unlock this model holder without triggering the alarm, but it's not generally known."

"There is?" she said. "What?"

"Extreme vibration, like an earthquake. The holder company says it's not a flaw, it's a feature." He stepped closer to the empty holster and bent to peer at it. "Impossible to tell if that's what happened her."

He straightened, and she saw the step that put him closer to the phone also put him closer to her. Dr. Light stood *right there*.

Her stomach lurched. Face to face, she didn't just see how big he was compared to her—she *felt* his dominance. If he were pack, he'd be alpha.

Even as a human, he was commanding. Her boss, their Techie Titan leader. Yes, he was definite geeky in his glasses and sweater vest. But he was techie royalty, their geek king.

She felt as if she should bow to him. Like a maiden of old, kneeling to her king.

Which would put her on the level for some interesting things if they were dating as well.

She realized her eyes must've been burning a hole in his abdomen...and drifting lower. She shot her gaze up to his face. He tipped a smile at her.

"Omniss had a good point," she blurted. Blushing, she rapped out, "Means, motive, and opportunity. It's almost certain the Wrapphone was taken while the store was closed. But I think he wasn't concentrating enough on motive. Sure, the employees could have done this—we all had means and opportunity. But who *would* have done this? Carol said nobody would cross you or Pan."

Dr. Light shrugged, and for a second she lost herself in the sheer beauty of his shoulder and arm muscles bunching and stretching. "It could be a disgruntled employee, wanting to get back at me. But I don't want it to be."

"Well, maybe the theft wasn't aimed at hurting you or Choice Buy. Maybe it's a Wrapphone competitor."

"Trying hurt the developer—or even to reverse-engineer the phone?"

He considered her, head tilted, a small smile on his lips. "You're smart, aren't you?"

She felt a blush of pleasure rise up her face. "I just like to consider all the possibilities." She'd learned that from the fiasco of attacking her mother's lover.

"That works. Sure better than one of my store family."

His family. Her insides twisted in longing. "Maybe it was just a random theft."

"Someone snatching up small, expensive toys he could sell for quick cash. Then why this phone, which was tethered, and only this phone?"

"You make a good point." She was surprised to see him straighten as if she'd fed his pride in return—as if he cared about her opinion of him as much as she cared about his of her. "Maybe the thief is one of us." She dared include herself in "us". "But working for an outsider."

"Industrial espionage?" He shook his head, firmly. "No. That I won't believe. Not my people. They might act out in rage against me. But my people won't stoop to federal offense."

"*Your* people. Yes. But..." She felt her cheeks heat. "But you didn't hire me."

"Carol did," he said with gratifying immediacy. "That's good enough for me. Besides, I knew you were right for us the moment I saw you facing product so efficiently."

"You saw me this morning?" She felt her eyes widen.

His cheeks stained with color. "Yes. I would have come over to introduce myself but...but..."

"But you had to rally the troops after being gone. I know." She smiled up into his eyes, so gorgeous behind his glasses. *He noticed me.* Miracles did occur. Maybe she hadn't imagined that dusting of masculine desire this morning, after he'd rescued her from the villainous falling television set. "So where does that leave us?"

"*Us?*" His color darkened, and he coughed. "Oh, where does that leave us with the *case*."

"Yes, that's what I meant." What did he think she meant. *Us*—him and her? Her inner wolf's tail started *whapping* at the thought. *Down, girl.*

"There is one more investigative string we can pull. If you have a few minutes."

"Sure." She liked that "we" entirely too much.

"The video surveillance caught something last night. I was going to look at it next. The program's on my computer in my office." He stepped over the tape and looked back at her. "Interested?"

*In being alone with you in your office? Very interested.* "Yes! I mean, yes. I'm very interested...in clearing my name."

He raised the tape with one hand and she ducked under.

"This way, then." With a cheery saunter, he led her toward the back area.

Emma followed, optimism bubbling inside. Sexy Gabriel Light was being nice to her. She would've been happy with him just not shoving her out the door. But he was including her in his investigation, inviting her into his office. *Maybe that even means he likes me...?* She took a quick, hopeful sniff.

The air trailing him curled into her nose. Headily male, overlaid by cotton twill and subtle, expensive cologne...

And nothing more. No extra testosterone, not even a hint of male desire.

She drooped. No matter how nice he was being to her, scent didn't lie.

He wasn't even remotely attracted to her.

Dr. Light keyed open his office door and led her inside. “Never had to constantly lock this before,” he muttered. “But Omniss insisted.” As she followed him in, he picked up the heavy guest chair like it was doll furniture, brought it around the back of the desk, and sat it beside his behemoth chair. “For you, m’lady.” He swiped a hand toward it with a quick bow and a mischievous smile. “You will not be harmed this time. I promise the dragon has gone for the day.”

She smiled back. Even if he didn’t *like*-like her, he was acting like he at least regular-liked her. “Thank you, m’lord.” She slid into the chair and dared ask a somewhat personal, “You game?”

“Absolutely. Just finished a campaign last night with my guildies. You?” Throwing himself into his own chair he grabbed his mouse and started clicking intently. With his other hand, he turned the large flat-panel monitor toward her.

“I used to. My new condo has pretty crappy wifi.” She leaned toward the monitor to see it better. A set of thumbnails cued up in neat rows and columns, each labeled a terse THE01, DVD03, CAR02, and the like. “Are those the security cameras?”

“Yes. This is the camera over the Wrapphone display.” He clicked on the thumbnail labeled PHO01. The screen filled with the main phone display area, customers dotted throughout. Center-picture, the Wrapphone was clearly visible on its stand. Carol stood beside it surrounded by half a dozen wide-eyed customers. Dr. Light right-clicked up a context menu, picked TIME from the menu, then when an entry popup displayed, rapidly touch-typed on the numeric keypad. “Between interviews, I ran the video from last night for Omniss, and we found this.”

The picture redisplayed with empty aisles. The time stamp was eleven p.m., the date the previous evening. Carol appeared briefly as if checking on the phone, then disappeared from the shot.

"The store alarm was armed a few minutes later. Then this happens."

A dark, skinny blob, like a hunched teen in black hooded fleece, slid into view. Emma drew in a breath, her hands clenching in her lap. The figure hovered there for several tense moments, swaying toward the phone as if drawn by it.

Then the top of the figure wobbled as if looking around. But the features were too blurry to see.

Suddenly the figure disappeared out of the shot.

*Like a frightened bunny,* Emma thought. "Who was that?"

"We don't know. The resolution isn't good enough to determine appearance or even gender, although from its build, I think it's a teenager."

"Not Brant," she said stoutly.

"Not Brant," he agreed with the flash of a grin. "For one thing, there was no product crashing to the floor."

She smiled into Dr. Light's crinkled, blue-green eyes. She couldn't help herself. He was sexy and smart and funny on top of it. Maybe he wasn't attracted to her, but it was all too easy to be attracted to him.

"I gave a copy to the police. Their expert is cleaning it up. But rather than wait for them to share their results..."

She felt her eyes widen in admiration. "You have a professional video editor?"

"I do." A sparkling male pride brightened his eyes. He turned back to the screen and clicked to stop the video.

The time, which had been running second-by-second on the bottom of the display, read eleven twenty.

It had started at eleven on the nose, and they'd been running the video in real time. Twenty minutes should have elapsed.

But it felt like only ten had gone by.

Being with Dr. Light made her feel giddy and time was wonky. But not missing-ten-minutes wonky.

He circled the mouse to click up another program.

"Wait." Without thought, she laid restraining fingers on his forearm. Sensations crashed into her. Warm skin. Crisp hair. Hard tendon. Harder muscle.

His gaze jerked toward her, his eyes wide and suddenly dark behind his glasses.

"Sorry!" Embarrassment wicked into her. She jerked back her hand. "Sorry. I'm sorry." Her voice didn't work quite right and the words were raspy.

"No, it's okay. You just startled me. What's wrong?"

"Not wrong, exactly, but...the time." She pointed.

He smiled. "You noticed the missing ten minutes? Nice. Omniss didn't have a clue."

Of course, Dr. Light had already noticed and cataloged the missing time long ago. The man was fearsomely smart.

Clicking up a complicated-looking video editor, he started working. "I think the thief fritzed the camera somehow—maybe an electromagnet pulse cannon—before he took the phone."

Emma sat there in stunned surprise. She'd nearly had an orgasm just from touching his naked skin and he'd been neither uncomfortable nor offended. She took a hopeful little sniff...but no, he still wasn't attracted either.

Still, he'd been impressed she'd noticed the ten minutes missing from the security video. *If I can't win his affection, at least I can probably win his respect*. And that was almost as good, right?

Once her heart settled down, she got absorbed watching Dr. Light finesse the advanced video editor.

A couple minutes later he gave a final, satisfied click. "That should do it."

Clicking back to the surveillance video, he ran it again. The dark blob slid on-screen, not so blobbish now.

Emma leaned closer. That was definitely a person in a hoodie.

"I'll slow it down so we can see detail." Dr. Light clicked and the seconds ticked by slower.

The figure leaned toward the Wrapphone...and suddenly straightened, glancing from side to side. That wobble had definitely been the guy checking out his surroundings. Maybe he'd heard something.

On one of the swivels, he turned his face toward the camera.

Young, male. Bottom half darkened with the scruff of an incomplete beard. Top half pale and frightened, nose twitching, the prey's instinctive sensing of a predator nearby.

The boy rabbited out of the shot.

Emma sat back. "What do you think scared him?"

"You caught that too?" He nodded. "Whatever it was, it was off camera. I checked the other angles but didn't find anything. Did you recognize him?"

"No. Are you going to show this version to Omniss or the police?"

"I'd give it to the police, but they can't use it. I'm a suspect too."

"No! That's terrible."

"Thanks for defending me, but actually, I'm glad. They'll have their own expert clean up the video. If I were their expert, I'd have to testify in court."

"And Omniss?"

His mouth flattened in that thin line she'd seen before. "Why bother? He's already made up his mind it's one of us."

"Me," she said sadly.

"He's an idiot. But trying to convince him otherwise is futile at this point. Like trying to jackhammer concrete—with my face." As she laughed, he added, "I saw this kid." He thumped the screen.

Her laugh imploded in surprise. "You did? Where? When?"

"Today. Slinking out of the store just as the first customers came in at nine. I think he hid out in the bathrooms until after closing. Maybe trying to steal a couple phones or a batch of the latest movies. I think whatever happened last night spooked him. But I'm hoping he's our thief."

"Why?"

"Because I think he'll be back tonight." He took out what looked like an exact replica of the Wrapphone. "And I think we can trap him."

# Chapter Seven

Emma left the Choice Buy that night with her emotions in turmoil. She'd been accused of theft and was one step closer to losing her job.

But she'd also connected with Gabriel Light on some level.

She walked toward the bus stop. Her current pack lived in a compound disguised as a condo community an hour away from Muskegon. Great for privacy to run as a wolf, but not so many jobs, so the pack subsidized a couple of busses into the city, running hourly on the three-quarter hour.

As she approached the shelter, she mulled it over.

Gabriel Light the man was physically a king, though he hid it well under those glasses and casual loose clothes. That was enough to get her wolf panting.

But every new thing she learned about her boss made him even more attractive.

Reaching the shelter, she sank onto a half-full bench seat to wait for the next bus.

He was brave, rescuing her from the evil falling TV monster. He was kind, understanding on some level that she needed to be involved in finding proof she wasn't the thief. He was courageous, yelling at the nasty Omniss on her behalf. He was sexy, making her wolf wag its tail—and want to lift it.

He was hella smart. That last appealed to her human most.

Everything about him seemed to call to something in her. Though he seemed to like her okay, she didn't smell any indication his "like" could ever be anything more.

The bus rumbled toward her. She popped to her feet with sudden determination.

Gabriel Light wasn't attracted to her. So what? She was a wolf. She could change that, given enough time.

Which meant keeping her job, and keeping his respect.

The bus stopped, the door opening with a hiss. As she boarded amid a scattering of second-shift workers, her determination firmed.

She'd be the best damned Techie Titan trainee he'd ever seen.

* * *

She floated in twilight's mists when the deep voice, filled with yearning, turned her. "Emma."

Her own body ached with longing in response, echoing and shimmering in her belly.

Her boss, Gabriel Light, stood there, normal from the waist down, hands in his slouchy pants' pockets. But from the waist up...

He was naked. And glorious.

*It's a dream.*

*Don't care.*

She let her gaze feast on him. Pectorals jutted under the wings of his collar bones. Abs marched like perfect little hillocks down the middle of his stomach. The short glinting hairs feathered there were just enough to remind her he was very, very male. Ropes of muscle banded his waist, just above the pants, which were suddenly much lower-slung than before, revealing a hint of a darker, shadowy patch.

And the scent of testosterone and male desire filled the air like smoky incense.

She shuddered in deep lust.

"Wh-what do you want?" Dream, yes, but it felt so real. She didn't want to screw things up.

"You." As if teleported, he was standing before her, all that glorious sleek skin just a reach away—with her tongue.

He reached for her chin, taking it between forefinger and thumb. The warm, male skin made her want to rub her face against his hand and rumble her happiness.

He bent, and his mouth found—no, took—hers.

His tongue thrust boldly into her mouth, conquering any doubts. Pleasure flooded her. He tasted of power and lust and strangely of magic. Or maybe that was just her innate magic rising to meet the call of its alpha.

Because alpha he was, her boss and her king, if only her geek king. In this dreamscape they were standing, and then they were lying down on a bed like soft clouds. He tore off her salmon-pink polo shirt, threw it to one side, and grabbed her nape in one strong, big hand.

He kissed her, lots of tongue, thrusting. Possessing.

His hand closed on her breast. Encasing the whole mound. Two fingers parted to let her nipple peep through, closed, then very, very gently pinched.

She shuddered to her core. He was taking her like a wolf. Dominating her with love and passion. Every particle of her responded with hard lust.

"I can't wait." He threw her onto her back. Rising to his knees over her, he stripped off her pants and panties with one hard yank. Somehow it made him naked too. His erection jutted proudly from thighs so thickly muscled they were as big as her torso. She wanted to wrap her legs around one of those hard trunks and rub herself ragged.

"Emma. You're everything I've ever wanted." His breathing was ragged. "Everything I've ever needed. Open for me, darling." He seized her hips, lifted her to him, and thrust himself home.

He took her like a wolf. As he drove into her over and over, she contracted to a diamond-hard point.

He took her like an alpha wolf. He fell onto her, his weight deliciously heavy, and thrust even deeper.

"Emma." He lifted his head to look into her eyes. His own, without glasses, were like novas lapped by summer seas, filled with desire, intense happiness...and love.

Oh God. He was taking her like a *mating* wolf.

She orgasmed hard, as if leaping through a stained glass window, shattering into a thousand thousand colored pieces, sparkling in the sunlight.

Emma woke shuddering, heart pounding in her ears, her thighs splashed with her glistening desire and satisfaction. Flopping onto her back, she flopped an arm over her eyes.

What an impossible dream. She'd only known him a day, and yet she'd dreamed of Gabriel loving her like a destined mate.

*Gabriel.* As if she'd ever get that close to him in real life. As if he'd ever desire her with that naked, aching yearning.

*Make* him want her, right. That was the impossible dream.

She curled around her pillow and bit back tears.

# Chapter Eight

The late night plus the dream plus worry over Omniss meant Emma slept poorly and, despite her determination to be impressive, she woke fuzzy and late. She had to skip breakfast, barely made the bus, and carded herself in after three failed swipes. Groggy, missing her morning coffee, she stumbled inside—into Dr. Light's broad chest.

Adrenaline flash-flooded her system at being so close to his broad, muscular torso. She fell back with a sucked-in breath. His distinct sexy scent sent her heart rate skyrocketing.

She adjusted her gaze a little higher. His star-shot blue-green eyes were warm behind his glasses as if he saw her reaction and sympathized. "I didn't sleep all that well either. I'm making a coffee run to Caffeine Addiction." He named the coffee shop in their strip mall. "What do you drink?"

It reminded her of her fantasy, inviting him out for coffee, then dinner, then a little hot man-on-shifter action. She blushed. "I'm fine," she blurted. "I mean, there's coffee in the break room. That's fine."

"If you slept like I did"—and there was that word slept again, almost demanding a "with me" to be added—"coffee *Vulgaris* isn't going to do it. C'mon, Emma, we're going to be here all night again. What do you want?"

She clenched her eyes briefly against him and her, together all night, and what she *wanted*. "You have a plan? To trap the thief, I mean?"

"I do. But I'm not sharing until you tell me your caffeine preference. Cappuccino? Mocha? Latte?"

"Just plain coffee," she blurted. "But...um, if they have any of those chocolate chunk cookies?"

He rewarded her with a huge smile. "You got it."

"I'll pay you back..."

He stopped her simply by glaring.

Her belly shimmied. So powerful, so alpha. It reminded her that, though Gabriel Light was kind, generous, protective, and mostly laid-back, he could be very dangerous.

"...or maybe not."

"Definitely not." Spinning on his heel, he left.

* * *

He returned with a carrier wafting a heavenly rich-bitter scent and two bags stamped with the Caffeine Addiction logo. The mouth-watering odor of chives and sharp cream cheese wafted from one bag, and the other was redolent of butter, sugar, and chocolate. Emma took an appreciative sniff, her wolf sighing in pleasure.

He set the carrier down on a break room table. "Sit. Enjoy your breakfast."

"I should be working—"

"You will. If you're worried about impressing your boss, only think– you'll be twice as efficient if you digest properly." He gave her an impish grin.

She could think of better ways to "impress" her boss. But she was suddenly hungry and realized if she sat to eat, maybe he would too.

Maybe he'd sit down and eat with her.

"I got another Wrapphone prototype rush-delivered. It's our bait for tonight."

"That's brilliant!" She sat.

And to her rising excitement, he began to sit down too. So, maybe not lovers like the dream, but on their way to friends?

Before she could do more than hope, Omniss's thin voice cut through.

"*Mr.* Light." The insurance adjuster appeared in the break room doorway. "We have work to do. You can eat later."

Her spirits dropped.

Her boss privately rolled his eyes at her but dutifully straightened and faced the man. "I'll eat when I need to. But I can work while I do." He snatched his cup from the tray and one of the paper bags. Hesitated. Leaning slightly toward Emma, he murmured, "I meant it. Take what time you need. You'll make up any hours on that special project."

Grateful, Emma watched him walk away, all broad shoulders and tight glutes, and she shuddered privately with lust.

The cookie impressed her–the biggest chocolate chunks she'd ever seen, he must've asked specifically for it–that reminded her she was going to try to impress him too, by being the best damned Techie Titan trainee there was.

Cramming the rest of her cookie in her mouth, she rose, picked up her coffee, and slurped it down on her way out of the break room.

Another employee was cleaning up the phone accoutrements aisle so she took herself to Base and pulled a work order. Laptop with virus symptoms. Easy-peasy. She'd disinfect it with Dr. Light's detox program, slap on an Internet security package and have it done in a flash.

Settling down in the back, she booted the computer off a CD with Dr. Light's specialized program. It went to work right away, scrubbing off verified double nasties, flagging other possibles.

Fingertips twinkling on the keyboard, quick wrist on the mouse, she began checking the possibles. Click, okay. Click, not okay and whisk to trash. She was a cleaning monster. She happily clicked, doing an amazing job cleaning.

*And yay, here comes Dr. Light—can't wait until he sees how well I'm doing...what's this?*

She clicked up a picture, tilting her head to try to make sense of what was going on.

*What are those people doing?* She tilted her head one way then the other, and still couldn't tell. It looked like a naked game of Twister, but instead of right leg or left arm...well, yeah. Defied the imagination.

"What's that, Emma?" Brant asked brightly.

Emma startled. Her wolf's hearing was exceptional but she'd been so distracted by the picture she hadn't heard the teen come up.

He leaned closer. "What's that man doing?"

"Shh." Her face heated. "Not so loud."

"Wow, that lady's flexible." If anything, the "not so loud" got his volume to open-road levels. "I didn't think you could put your ankles behind your ears like that." He shook his head admiringly.

Which was of course when Dr. Light glided around the privacy barrier. "Brant, there you are. Carol wants to see you."

"Okay, Dr. Light. But maybe you can tell me. What's that?" He pointed at Emma's screen.

"What's what?" Dr. Light leaned over to look.

"Nothing!" Emma slapped the laptop shut. Any cleaning was negated. She'd have to start over, and her visions of amazing metrics died.

"Are you okay?" Dr. Light reached for her shoulder, as if to touch it reassuringly, but at the last minute he hesitated and his fingers only hovered.

"I'm fine."

"Well...all right. We'll get out of your hair. Brant, come on."

* * *

Though Gabriel was going to trap the thief in person, he wanted the security camera footage as backup. However the culprit had screwed up the camera last time—most likely an EMP cannon, but he couldn't rule out a witch using magic to fritz the camera—he needed to armor against it.

He spent most of the day working on a tech/charm meld to protect against either. An hour before the store closed, he went to each of the store's security cameras, touched the special talisman he'd created, and waved a surreptitious hand in the camera's direction.

Then he found Carol in the break room.

His second assistant manager was going over employee schedules. He paused. She usually locked up. Though it wasn't unheard of for him to do it, he knew she was on edge because she felt the police considered her a prime suspect. So he had to seem absolutely natural telling her she could go home.

Time to get into the right frame of mind. Tell Carol casually that he'd lock up. She'd ask why. *To spend time with Emma, alone, to be together with her, potentially all night. Talking with her, smelling her, touching her, kissing her, fucking her into the floor...*

Gritting his teeth, he willed down his erection. Absolutely natural? Try just not walking with a planky hitch.

"Dr. Light?" She looked up, startled. "Do you need something?"

"You can go home now, Carol. I'll lock up." He couldn't quite keep his excitement from his voice, but he didn't think it showed too badly.

The way her expression twisted with worry, he was wrong. "Is there something I should know, Dr. Light?"

"No, nothing. Not really." He scrambled to ease her mind. "I've got an idea regarding the theft I'm testing."

Her shoulders loosened and she smiled. "You and your tests. You should have been a scientist."

Well, he was, but not in the way she meant it. Ever since his parents died in a magically induced plane crash, his life's goal was to make magic and tech work together. It meant he was an expert in both magic and science.

He only smiled back. "Thanks."

Emma had left the store at her normal time, but Gabriel knew she was waiting in the nearby sandwich shop until closing. Once Carol was safely out the front door, he strode to the back employee entrance to let her in without her card. That way, if anything should go wrong, only he would be officially on the hook.

His stomach bubbled as he moved from stride to trot to almost a dash. He hadn't been this excited since he'd gotten his first real wand.

And to think, when the Wrapphone prototype had been stolen, he'd been angry. He'd expected to be in the store when it arrived so he could secure the thing with magic, or put a psychic eye on it so he could trace it. But it had arrived early, while he was troubleshooting out of state.

But now, some part of him was actually glad it had been stolen. It gave him a chance to spend time with Emma.

*Ms. Singer.*

Oh, hell. He could call her Emma in his mind, right?

At the back entrance, he glanced out the reinforced window beside the shipping docks. There she was on the pad, hands in her pockets, bouncing on her toes. Bubbling with excitement too? It notched his up.

Or cold? June still got chilly at night. Immediately he chastised himself and threw open the door. "Come in." He barely stopped himself from taking her arm and drawing her inside. He wanted her warm and safe...and he had an inexplicable need to touch her.

But that would lead to other, potentially headsmen-involving things. He simply stood aside and let her pass before him.

Her scent drifted, siren-like, into his nose. Sweet and sassy and above all, female. His cock rose with interest. He clenched his eyes and jaw briefly and willed the thing down.

"Is the new Wrapphone still in place?" she said in a low voice as she peeled off her jacket.

"Yes." He'd made a replica of the phone—with magic, but he didn't tell her or anyone that. Nobody could know it was fake.

"Good thing the developer had that backup."

"And was willing to rush deliver it, yes." Gabriel had put the news on their website and posters in the windows announcing they'd gotten a second Wrapphone, then locked the thing onto the stand this morning. As bait, he hoped it would prove impossible to ignore.

In a low voice she said, "Do you think the thief is here?"

"Yes. On my final sweep, one of the men's room stalls was almost shut. But we need to let him come out in his own time."

"We need to catch him in the act, I get it."

And she did. As he set the building alarm, he reflected on the joy of being with someone who really listened to what he said.

They hunkered down in the shadows just outside the phone display cutout area.

While they waited, she said quietly, "So you game. Role-playing?"

"Mostly," he murmured in return. They should have stayed silent but it was too much fun being with her. "I have some match-3 and card games on my phone for waiting in lines."

"Me, too." She began chatting about her favorites, naming many of his.

He relaxed so much, he said without thinking, "Hey Emma. Schröding's cat walks into a bar. And doesn't."

Mentally, he face-palmed. That was such a geek joke. *Smooth first-date material, Light.* Nobody ever got it, and most people didn't even know it was a joke...

She *laughed.* "Tell me another."

His spirits did a one-eighty. She'd probably only pretended to find it funny, but so what? He'd take it. "Okay. Have you heard of the band named 1023 Megabytes? They haven't had any gigs yet. Ba-dum-bum." He mimed a cymbal rimshot.

She stared at him, and he crumpled inside. That one was so weird she couldn't even pretend...and then her face collapsed into a huge grin, eyes scrunching, and she snorted a long laugh. "No gigs. Like gigabyte, 1024 meg. Ha."

He stared at her, disbelieving. He'd once told his sister that his true love would be the woman who loved his sense of humor. She'd responded tartly that he meant the woman who loved him *in spite* of his sense of humor.

Emma actually enjoyed his jokes. Not the cold shoulder or blank non-understanding or forced laugh other women gave.

And then she said, "Okay, I've got one. A Roman walks into a bar and holds up two fingers." She demonstrated, holding her pointer and middle in a V." He says, Five beers, please.'"

"Roman numeral five, ha." Slightly dizzy, he quipped back, "How do you tell the difference between a chemist and a plumber?"

"Ask them to pronounce unionized," she laughed. "Un-ionized!"

He grinned at her, feeling like he was glowing from the inside. She not only got and enjoyed his humor, she returned his puns.

*Keeper.*

He shook the thought away with a casual, “Oh, you have a little something on your shirt.” He plucked the end of a single hair from her shoulder—just as a scuffing from the back made Emma grab his wrist. She exchanged a wide-eyed glance with him. He nodded, sliding the hair into his pocket.

Their perp was here.

# Chapter Nine

Emma rose to a crouch while Dr. Light unfolded silently beside her. They were sheltered in the shadows of the DVD/entertainment aisle kitty-corner across from the phones, a sales bin providing extra cover. She peeped out from behind the bin.

A dark, lanky form crept toward the display area, hooded head swiveling. Emma's breath sucked in. She barely stopped herself from punching the air in victory. *Yes.* The thief was here.

Beside her, Dr. Light practically vibrated with intensity, his whole being on-point to catch the thief—like a wolf scenting prey. He'd be one hell of a hunt-mate.

Her whole body whooshed at the thought. Her wolf lolled its tongue and panted happily. She shushed them both.

The thin boy sidled up to the fake Wrapphone. He put a hand on it...slid it from the stand...drew it out...and suddenly stopped. The lock cable. She watched, breath held, for him to unlock it.

He yanked. The phone stayed tight. He yanked again, more flustered. Quickly growing angry. The phone was still attached. Dr. Light exchanged a quick, puzzled look with her.

If this kid had taken the real Wrapphone, he'd know how to release the cable.

But the kid made a frustrated growl, pulled out a switchblade knife, and tried to saw through the cable. An extended moment of shrieks and swears made Emma, with her sensitive hearing, wince.

The kid raised the knife to his hooded face. Its edge was wrecked.

Just then the air conditioning kicked in.

The kid startled. Emma's held breath came out in a rush. The kid, either spooked by the air or hearing Emma's hiss, ran.

"Crunchy damn." Dr. Light took off after him.

The man was fast, but the boy had a head start. She could see Dr. Light wouldn't catch him, so she shifted to wolf. Her father had explained once that, as creatures of magic, the shift was really more like exchanging one body for the other, and so the clothes that were on her as a human would still be on her when she shifted back. The stronger the shifter's magic, the easier and faster the shift, and the more nuanced, like Emma's ability to change out individual parts of her body.

As wolf, she bounded off down a parallel aisle. Extending her forelegs and pushing with her powerful hindquarters, she sped up until she saw the boy in flashes between gaps in the counters. She was gaining...gaining... Just before the far wall, she caught up.

She leaped for him, shifting human midair, and tackled the boy to the ground. Small in both woman and wolf forms, the thief outweighed her by a good fifty pounds. But with her momentum, she took him down.

"Good job, Emma!" Gabriel Light crowed, running up.

The kid was already struggling beneath her. Shoving her off, he scrambled to his feet, about to run again.

Dr. Light grabbed the would-be thief by the shoulder, the man's strong fingers digging through hoodie and shirt to cinch on muscles underneath, by the boy's wince.

Dr. Light grimaced. "Sorry if I'm pinching you, but you might shrug the hoodie off and run again. What were you doing?"

"Nothing." The boy cast a surly glance out of his dark cocoon.

Dr. Light pushed the hood back. The boy was a scrawny seventeen if he was a day, younger even than Brant. "Did you take the original Wrapphone last night?" Dr. Light touched a hand to his waist, and strangely, the boy relaxed.

Even more strangely, he began to talk.

"Last night, I hid until closing. I was gonna take a few small things, to sell. You're rich, you wouldn't miss them."

Dr. Light's jaw tightened but he didn't say anything.

"Then I saw a man come in." It was the only time the boy's narration got excited. "Through a wormhole or something! Like a tunnel that just appeared midair, and this robed man stepped out."

Emma breath hitched. *That sounds like witch magic.* She didn't know a lot about magic, just the basics, that shifters were magic, witches did magic, and familiars knew magic—but the biggie was that mundanes could never ever find out about magic. The Witches' Council had jailed shifters over that.

She glanced at Dr. Light, who rolled his eyes reassure-ingly.

Well, of course. She didn't know a lot about Gabriel Light, but she did know he had a scientific mind. He'd reject even the idea of magic.

"All right." Dr. Light's doubt dripped on every word. "What then?"

The kid grimaced. "He swiped the pricey phone."

"How'd he open the lock?"

The kid made a vague circling gesture. "He spun his hand at it, and then it shook, harder and harder, until it just sort of popped open."

Emma didn't know why, but the idea of magic became more firmly planted in her brain.

"I see." Dr. Light grimaced. "What's your name?"

The teen's jaw kicked up belligerently. "Raider."

"Your real name."

"Tanner," he grumbled. "But everyone uses my street name."

"We're not on the street right now. Follow me, Tanner. If you try to run, I'll make it worse for you." He released the teen and, waving Emma into step with him, led the way to the break room.

Again, strangely, the boy simply did as he was told.

On the way, Dr. Light leaned toward Emma. "Do you believe him?"

Emma could smell lies pouring off humans. This boy had only smelled of boy, and cheap cologne. "Yes. Or at least, I believe he believes it."

"All right. Tanner, sit there." He pointed at a table and began to feed coins into the vending machine. Gathering an armful of bags, he dumped them in front of the boy. "Eat. You can sleep tonight in my office. Tomorrow, you work here to make up for the trouble you caused."

At that, some of the boy's belligerence came back. "You gonna pay me?"

"Pay you?" A light entered Dr. Light's eyes. "If you work hard—yes."

The teen blinked in surprise...and strangely, a bit of hope bled through into his gaze.

"Now. Tell me the most important thing." Dr. Light settled a soft drink can in front of the boy, who was ripping into the bags and stuffing food in his mouth like he was starving.

And maybe he was. The boy glared sullenly as he filled his mouth, barely chewing to say, "What?"

"Why did you do it?"

And then Gabriel Light *waited.* Patiently, calmly.

Emma gazed at his strong profile with admiration. Most wolves would simply rip answers from their suspect.

Dr. Light...didn't.

Quietly, she lowered herself into a chair and waited too, fascinated to see how this played out.

"Why?" The boy snorted as he finally slowed down. "Because that's the only way. You wouldn't understand."

One dark eyebrow raised in challenge.

"You wouldn't," the boy repeated. After another couple seconds of that eyebrow, the teen spat, "It's my gang. Or not *my* gang." He grimaced, as if he'd revealed too much.

*Not* his *gang?* The gang he wanted in on, then, but was only peering in from the outside?

Like she was with her family. Poor boy. He'd need to prove himself. Aching for him, for herself, she said, "You thought stealing would prove to them you belong."

The teen's sullen gaze switched to her and lit with surprise. "Yeah."

"Why do you need a gang?" Dr. Light asked gently. "Don't you have a family? Friends?"

"Family?" The boy laughed bitterly. "It's *because* of my family I need the gang. I need the steady income, you know? To buy my mom's meds...shit. I want a lawyer."

He shut down, but Emma's heart went out to him. *We're only trying to please people...because nobody really wants us.* She'd alienated her mother and brother; she'd been trying to make up for that incident ever since. Trying to win her way back into her family's hearts.

This boy was trying to make room for himself, too.

"Lawyers are for police interrogation. You've already told me everything I need to know. Done eating? Take your soda pop and come with me. I'll show you where you can bed down. Emma..." His blue-green eyes came to her, and his expression was torn.

"It's okay. I'll let myself out."

Behind his glasses, his gaze intensified. "I'd rather walk you to the bus stop and wait with you."

"But you can't." She knew he couldn't leave the boy on his own. "I'll be fine. See you tomorrow?"

"Tomorrow." He smiled gratefully. "We'll talk then."

* * *

When she came out, the bus stop was empty of life. She sat down on the bench and breathed a deep sigh.

The smell of spoiled meat floated on the air from the nearby sandwich store. They must've just thrown the stuff into their dumpster.

She sighed again.

Suddenly the prissy little insurance adjuster, Omniss, appeared.

"Ah-hah! I've caught you now."

Emma, deep in her own head, blinked up at the insurance adjuster in confusion. "What are you doing here?"

"That idiot detective suspected the assistant manager. Sure, she was the only one to demonstrate the phone, and she was the last one in the building the night it disappeared. But I knew better. And sure enough, when the new Wrapphone came in, it was too good to pass up. I *knew* I'd catch you."

Emma was tired from stress and long days and she'd just had the most amazing time of her life with the most amazing man she'd ever met, only to have it cut short. She was not in the mood for Omniss. "Whoopee. You caught me catching the bus."

"No, I've caught you coming out of the Choice Buy after the alarm was set. No doubt for more nefarious deeds."

"I didn't take anything."

"We'll see about that."

"What do you mean by that?" She nearly snarled it.

He took one surreptitious step back. "I think a body search will prove quite interesting."

Just as a patrol car prowled into the strip mall parking lot.

# Chapter Ten

Emma watched the patrol car pull to the curb, incredulous. Who had Omniss bribed to get the police here? She protested, “I didn’t take the Wrapphone.”

“We’ll let the cops determine that.” Omniss seized her arm and yanked her toward the car. The smell from the sandwich shop came stronger.

She could have used her wolf's animal strength to resist, but when her iota got angry, Emma sometimes lost control, as the Bloodfang fiasco with her mother had proved. Emma didn’t trust her wolf not to take a dollar-fifty of Omniss’s best hamburger out of him.

So she went quietly and an hour later, she was sitting in holding cell waiting for a female police officer to come and do the search. From what she’d overheard, she’d be waiting until morning.

Alone.

Her shoulders hunched and she wanted to cry. She’d been so happy getting the Choice Buy job. It had felt so nice working with Dr. Light. She’d felt almost as if she belonged.

It had all backfired. Now she sat here, potentially worse off than before. Even when the police found she didn't have the Wrapphone on her, Omniss seemed to be determined to prove she was the thief. And how long would Dr. Light want her as an employee if she'd been in prison?

Alone. She lay back on her bunk. Or rather, alone *again*. She ought to be used to it by now, ought to relish it, even. After all, there were so many things she could do better alone. Use her wolf's nose to investigate. Use her wolf to run after the thief.

But with a partner like Gabriel Light...she could think of so much more to do *not* alone. Waiting. Jokes. Smelling his masculine essence. Basking in his alpha presence.

Sex.

She shivered with longing. She'd probably never have sex with him—he was too big and smart and her boss and human—but if she could, even once, she just knew it would be amazing.

She lay back on her bunk, remembering her dream, and imagined them trying to fit together. He towered over her. He'd have to bend to kiss her, whereas her mouth...was just about nipple level. She could lick and kiss the mounds hidden by his sweater vest to her heart's content.

No, she'd tear off that damned vest and lick his naked body like ice cream. Heat pooled in her belly, down low.

He'd fondle her breasts. And how would that feel?

Cracking her eyes, she double-checked there were no cameras before touching her breast, plucking at the nipple, imagining him doing it. His fingers would be big, hot, and oh-so-capable.

Her hands could roam over his ribs and the flare of his lats to his back. Wrapping her arms around his trunk, they'd rest easily on his waist, her hands sliding down his glutes without having to stretch. She could nibble down his hillock abs and would barely have to bend to take his growing erection into her mouth. She wondered how big he'd be, straining for her.

Or maybe he'd lift her to wrap her thighs around his hips. She'd be light and he'd be strong enough. He'd kiss her, slide his hands under her bottom to cup her buttocks. She'd rub herself against him, growing hot and wet between her thighs, rumpling the hair of his body as she clung to him and tasted him.

She slid a hand into her pants and met her raised, hard clit. One stroke took her finger sliding inside her. Her sex was hot, wet, and swollen open. She trembled. Completely ready so fast, just from thinking about him.

She'd feel his erection growing beneath her and swivel her hips to pop him into place. He'd slip easily into her blossoming sex and it would take one hard thrust of hips, his or hers, to drive him deep inside her.

*Uh.* Her body shuddered with lust, wringing her pelvis with deep need.

She'd gasp. He'd drive his tongue into her open mouth and take pleasure in her. He'd be big for her mouth but he'd give her pleasure in return, driving his tongue into her in tandem with his pistoning cock. He'd hold her steady with one brawny arm wrapped around her, his hand clamped to her hips, holding her still for his driving cock, thrusting over and over, pushing her higher and higher until she peaked...

She barely remembered possible ears in time, coming so hard it was almost impossible to throttle her moan, but she managed to swallow most of it.

As her thudding heart slowed and her body cooled, she withdrew her hand. That had been the best orgasm she'd ever had.

She could only imagine what the real Gabriel Light would be like.

* * *

Gabriel went to retrieve the fake Wrapphone. Returning to his office, he locked the phone in his desk drawer then sat in his executive chair, his gaze lighting on the sleeping boy.

Without the teenage belligerence or the boy's worries twisting his face, he looked even younger than sixteen or seventeen. Gabriel sighed.

A vibrating came from his belt. He sighed again. He'd have explained it away as his phone to anyone who noticed, but it was actually one of his talismans, signaling it needed a recharge. He knew which one. The scent-absorber, working overtime to neutralize the scent of his desire for Emma.

The talisman's low-power-alert had already been vibrating earlier, or he might have tried to keep her here longer on some excuse. Pulling it out from under his sweater vest, he saw it blinking red. Nearly empty.

Wow. Should've lasted a whole week, but gone in couple days? He rarely put a power alert on his talismans, but he was glad he took the extra trouble for this one.

Time to make more.

The way he'd reacted to her, time to make a lot more.

Rising, he activated a simulacrum of himself in the chair, then sketched a quick screen spell between his credenza and where the teen slept. If the boy woke, he'd only see Gabriel doing paperwork.

Releasing the hide on his equipment, Gabriel took down a half-dozen talisman blanks.

His hand closed on a bracelet blank.

Permanent hires got a comprehensive benefits package including a free emergency bracelet engraved with allergies, medical conditions, and a toll-free number to call if they were in trouble—plus one added benefit. A touch of magic. If the employee felt him- or herself in immediate danger, Gabriel's phone would chirp an alert. Thanks to basic human nature, he got an alarm from one employee or another a couple times a month.

Normally he'd wait until the probationary period was up to make the bracelet. But as long as he had his equipment out, he'd create Emma's.

*Ah, crunchy hell, be honest. I'm going to do everything I can to make her permanent.*

He wasn't sure if he meant employment or something more.

As he set up for the neutralizers first, he thought about what Tanner had said. If the boy was to be believed, a man had stepped from a mid-air tunnel.

That sounded suspiciously like a witch.

A witch changed everything. Emma's shifter nature would protect her from ordinary crooks, but a mage's battle? He didn't want her exposed to that.

Conclusion—he'd have to set the next trap alone.

*If* it was a witch. He set his small cauldron over a tea light, snapped his fingers, and lit the fire. Witches and tech went together like vinegar and paper cuts. The more finicky the tech, the worse the misfires. Seriously, a normal witch could never use something as advanced as the Wrapphone, at least, not reliably.

A mundane with a tunneling talisman? That made more sense technically, but most mundanes didn't know the secret of magic.

Unless it was a shifter or familiar.

*Not Emma.*

Grimacing, he plunked the blanks into the cauldron and picked up a lancet. Not for blood magic, but a drop would key the talismans to his scent. He pricked himself then watched the ruby liquid gather and fall.

*Be honest. Logically, it could be her.* She needed the money and had smarts and guile enough to evade Carol's sweep that first night. Emma was definitely smart enough to figure out how to get a cable lock opener and use gloves. More, as a shifter, she'd not only know about witches, she'd probably have access to one. Sure, packs didn't like witches, but someone had to make the talismans and spells that guarded their ceremonial grounds.

Still, his whole being rebelled against the idea. *Not Emma.*

Smart and capable, she'd also proved herself to be kind, conscientious, and a hard worker. Not that Omniss would care about any of that. With a soft snarl, he took out his wand and waved an incantation over the cauldron. Something would have to be done about Omniss.

He let the talismans simmer and picked up the bracelet.

Extracting the single hair he'd filched from her earlier, he wrapped it around the links. He plucked a couple of his own from his scalp and tucked them under hers. Murmuring an incantation, he waved his wand over the bracelet, flicking the wand on the last word to fuse the hairs' essence into the bracelet with hot bonding magic.

The hairs didn't light, they exploded.

*Emma's in trouble.* His heart nearly exploded with the hair. She was in trouble *now*.

Gabriel was rarely rash, but that did it. He waved a quick hide spell over his equipment, snatched up the bracelet, frisbee'd a business card with his cell phone number onto the sleeping boy in case he woke, and dashed for the door. Almost immediately he wheeled, blew out the tea light, used his fingers to fish out the no-scent talismans, ouching them into his pocket as he ran out the door.

# Chapter Eleven

"Ms. Singer, you're free to go. But stay in the Muskegon area."

Surprised, Emma rose as the officer opened the cell. She'd used her one phone call to contact her new alpha, but she was a mere iota. She thought he'd wait until morning to send her a lawyer. And she expected it to take at least a day for the lawyer to arrange her release.

The last face Emma expected to see was Gabriel Light's. But at the rush of relief and gratitude she felt, she knew it was exactly the face she'd needed to see.

"Dr. Light!" She hurried toward him, barely stopping herself from wrapping arms around him and clinging like a pup. "Mr. Omniss met me coming out of the store. He accused me of taking the Wrapphone."

"I know." His hand closed briefly around her upper arm, steadying her. "The man's an ass."

"How did you know I was here? Did he tell you he got me arrested?"

"Him? No."

"Then how did you find me?"

He jerked a shrug like his broad shoulders were really tight. "Omniss has police contacts. But I do, too." He left it at that, but his grim expression told her there was more to it.

He started out. She trotted after, his long-legged stride making her take three steps for every two of his. He really was quite tall.

He saw, and with a grimace, slowed.

"Well, thank you. I owe you."

"You don't owe me a thing." His grimace deepened. "I should've been monitoring the situation closer. This is my fault. Take the day off—with pay."

"I'm fine, Dr. Light." Did he not want her at the store? Embarrassed by her arrest? "Besides, what about Tanner's story? If he's telling the truth, he's not the thief. Which means the thief is still out there. We need to set another trap—"

"Look, I'm thinking maybe we should let the professionals handle it."

That hit her like a slap. "Dr. Light, is something wrong?"

"Wrong?" He laughed, no humor in it. "When we thought the thief was a boy, it was one thing. But if we're dealing with an adult with any kind of power at all..." He grimaced. "We need to step back. Let the police do their job."

"They did—and I got arrested," she said tartly.

He winced. They got to the doors and he automatically opened one for her. "I got you a taxi." Following her out, he pointed into the parking lot, where a cab idled. "It's prepaid."

She stopped to gape. “Dr. Light, I live in Scottville. That’s over sixty miles from here.” It would cost him big bucks.

He smiled wanly. “An apology for making you go through this.”

“You didn’t. Mr. Omniss did.”

He jerked a single-shoulder shrug. “We’ll agree to disagree about blame. Oh. Before I forget. This is for you.” He drew something shiny out of his pocket. “It’s not fancy. Stainless, not silver.” His tone was apologetic as he handed the thing to her.

It was a bracelet, the kind with medical alerts. She took it and saw her name engraved on one side, a phone number on the other. “What’s this?”

“All hires get one. Usually at the ceremony where we make you a permanent employee, but after what happened tonight, I thought...well, you can call that number for any trouble. Legal, car breaking down, whatever.”

“Thanks.” Did this mean he was thinking of hiring her permanently? Her spirits rose.

“But seriously. Don’t come in tomorrow. I mean today. Maybe stay home until this whole thing is over.”

And that made them plummet again. “Dr. Light, please don’t ask that of me. I can’t stand by and do nothing.” Emotions goosing her, she added, “It’ll drive me *nuts*.”

That surprised a laugh out of him. With a smile that turned sad, he said, “I don’t suppose you can.” He helped her into the cab. “Come in if you have to. But I’d rather you didn’t.”

As the taxi drove off, his words resonated in her head. *I’d rather you didn’t.*

* * *

Gabriel saw Emma off before climbing into his sports car and returning to the Choice Buy store. Her eyes had been hollow and her face pale. Her experience in lockup had obviously scared her and caused her a good deal of pain and grief.

He was going to flay Omniss alive for putting her through that—right after he caught the Wrapphone thief.

He knew her work ethic meant she was coming in, and he wasn't going to put her in harm's way again if he could help it. He let himself into the store and returned to his office.

To his relief, the boy Tanner was still snoozing on the couch, sprawled out on his back and gently snoring. He wondered if the kid didn't normally have a safe place to sleep.

Gabriel took the fake Wrapphone from his locked drawer. He'd already put a psychic eye on the phone, a sort of magical GPS. But if he was dealing with a witch, the eye was too easy to find and remove. So he layered a second psychic eye under the first—and hid it with a blanket mirror spell. "Take that, you son of a bitch," he murmured.

When Tanner woke around six a.m., Gabriel locked the bugged fake phone in his desk and took the teen out to a 24-hour diner for breakfast.

Tanner ate like one leg was hollow. Gabriel only smiled. He'd been like that at that age, too.

After breakfast, he stopped at a corner drug store to pick up hygiene supplies for the teen. Returning to the store, Gabriel handed the bag to the boy and showed him the bathroom. "Get cleaned up. You're going to work today, and you're going to work hard."

"But I get paid, right?" Again that poignant look in his eyes, of hope so often disappointed, piercingly sad to Gabriel.

"Don't trust me? Here's a twenty now." Gabriel took out his wallet and handed the boy a bill. "There'll be another one of those for every two hours you work."

"Really?" The boy's voice lit with amazement. Then he seemed to hear the eagerness in his own voice, and he slouched back with a feigned sneer. "Dunno if that's worth my time. I can make twice as much with the gang."

"Sure—but can you tell your mother where you got the money?"

Tanner blinked.

*Gotcha,* Gabriel thought with satisfaction. He'd see how the teen did today. Maybe, with time and patience, he'd be able to steer him toward a better path. "Get cleaned up."

Gabriel got the boy a trainee shirt. When his first assistant manager, Pan, came in for the day, he told him what had happened and asked him to keep the boy productively busy. Pan was also his panther familiar, and a wise creature.

Pan simply drawled, "Fine. But I get extra for this."

Then Gabriel took the fake bugged phone out of its locked drawer and set it on its stand.

Waiting for closing.

Emma arrived at her usual time. Despite not wanting her in harm's way, he felt a zing of pleasure seeing her.

Still, he couldn't afford her being here if the mage showed up. Resolutely he turned away. The little sag to her shoulders as he did knifed him in the chest. But it was for her safety.

Five p.m. came, and Pan brought the teen Tanner to him. His familiar nodded. Gabriel counted out four twenties and offered them to the boy. “If you come back tomorrow, there’s more.”

The eager light in the boy’s eye came again and got stronger.

“How’d he do?” Gabriel watched the teen leave, peeling out of his trainee shirt as he went. Patience, Gabriel reminded himself. Persistence, and much, much patience.

“The kid bitched. But he worked.”

“Okay. That’s as good as it gets, for now.”

“Oh—that ass Omniss came in just long enough to tell me to tell you not to expect his insurance company to cover your new Wrapphone.”

Gabriel snarled. “The coward knows I’d have decked him if I saw his face.”

“Yeah. I’m heading out. You coming?”

“Sure.” He walked with Pan out the front doors, then smacked his forehead with a palm. “I just forgot some paperwork. You go on without me.” Gabriel had prepared the lie ahead of time.

But even so, his familiar knew him too well. Pan arched a single black brow. “Right. Well, have fun.”

Gabriel returned to his office—where he instead hunkered down to wait. The thief hadn’t come last night—maybe because Gabriel had closed the store himself.

Better that Carol locked up anyway, seeing as she’d taken his offer last night as a sign that he mistrusted in her.

He snuck out around seven to get a bagel sandwich and coffee to go from the coffee shop. He almost wished he’d asked Emma to stay. She would have enjoyed coffee and a bagel with him. Almost as much as he’d enjoy her company.

But safety first.

Sneaking back into the store, he dodged employees, especially Carol, locked himself into his office, and gnawed at his dinner. Maybe nerves, maybe too much caffeine, but he put the paper cup and bagel aside, both half-finished.

When Carol did the all-call, he turned on his camera monitor software. He watched her arm the building's exterior alarms then leave.

Counting slowly to ten, he continued to watch the monitors, waiting in case she'd forgotten something and came back.

All was quiet.

He stole out to observe the phone area.

He started out crouching. Then, as his feet began to tingle with the lack of circulation, he slid onto his knees, then onto his butt. The day had been warm and the air condition system hadn't quite kept up with it. The ventilation system whirred. The heat and burr of sound made Gabriel drowsy. He was starting to nod off when he felt a rush of magic along his skin.

His eyelids shot up. The air stirred near the phones.

A magical portal whirl open.

A hooded, dark-robed man stepped through a few feet from the fake phone. Talismans hung around his neck like a livery collar. Gabriel silently slid his feet under himself, peering closer. Beneath the witch's hood...he was masked and wearing gloves.

Both magically and technically savvy? Sausage and egg McDamn.

The man gestured at the PHO01 security camera. Paused. Frowning, Gabriel readied his wand.

The witch circled his arm, hard and fast, barked "Break!"

A sudden shattering and tinkle of glass hitting carpeted concrete signaled every camera in the area bursting.

*Chocolate frosted fuck.* So much for Gabriel's camera protection spell. The witch was strong.

He touched his freeze spell amulet and whipped up his wand.

Just as Emma leaped from behind the DVD sales bin, dashing toward the masked mage.

# Chapter Twelve

Shock hit Gabriel, arresting his wand midair, as Emma dashed toward the unknown witch. She'd crept back in without him, Carol or Pan knowing? Brave...and foolish.

The mage touched a medallion on his collar then slashed his wand in a tight circle. Air seemed to solidify into a spear of wind.

*Air mage,* Gabriel thought. Hopefully, that was the only element the witch had. A royal witch like Gabriel, with power over multiple elements, was much, much more dangerous.

The witch jabbed his wand at Emma. The spear arrowed toward her.

She saw it coming and twisted mid-stride, trying to avoid getting impaled. She started falling, but Gabriel could already see she wouldn't get clear in time.

*Save her.* His mind went into overdrive. *Shield spell?*

No. Without knowing how strong that air spear was, or if it was reinforced with another element, he couldn't be sure his shield would hold. Besides, she'd see the spear bounce off a shield or bounce off it herself. With her quick brain, she'd know a second witch had protected her. Made it pretty obvious who.

He'd had countless opportunities to tell her the truth—and hadn't. She'd feel hurt, betrayed. Maybe worse.

If it had been the only way to protect her, if he was sure the shield would hold, he'd have done it in a heartbeat.

But Gabriel was a battle mage. He had plenty of options.

He slashed his wand, jetting pure magic on an intercept course with the spear, with a muttered, "Skew."

The enemy witch's spear hit Gabriel's magic—and slid sideways.

Gabriel bared his teeth in a savage grin. *Yes.*

The spear slammed straight into a display of high-end cameras.

*No.* Gabriel stifled a curse. His insurance company was going to have a fit.

The cameras exploded on impact. Plastic, glass, and computer chips spewed out, hitting the floor in a spatter of pricey tinkles.

He was already dashing for Emma as she tumbled to the floor—and rolled immediately onto her feet, launching herself again at the enemy witch.

But the witch had already flashed his wand at the fake Wrapphone with a rasped, "Tornado." A cyclone whipped up over the phone display.

The phone, stand, and cable shuddered violently in the whirling wind.

Touching a talisman under his vest, Gabriel triggered a clamp spell. He slashed out his wand, aiming the spell...

Just as Emma leaped for the fake phone.

Gabriel jerked his wand to one side. The clamp spell hit the phone next to the fake Wrapphone. He breathed a sigh of relief. *Whew, caught it in time.*

The clamp spell's momentum sent the phone slamming into the phone beside it. The two fused into a lump of useless plastic and metal.

More insurance claims. He could imagine the paperwork mounting up.

In a violent whirl of wind, the fake Wrapphone's stand vibrated so wildly the cable popped off—just as Emma thrust her hands into the tornado of wind.

"Emma, no!" Gabriel leaped for her. He would have grabbed her hands to pull them out of the damaging wind.

But he saw last minute her arms sprouting hair and her hands claws, as she called on her wolf's strength to clamp the phone to its stand. Gabriel marveled at her speed and ability to partially shift. He grabbed her shoulders instead, steadying her. She might be a small woman, but her wolf was strong.

The enemy witch snarled. Gabriel braced himself for a new attack.

Instead, the wind suddenly cut.

Emma stumbled. Gabriel's own feet stuttered. The witch shoved her, hard.

The phone popped from her fists.

"Ha!" The enemy witch made a pulling motion and the phone sucked into his hand. With a cackle of triumph, he dashed off.

"STOP!" Emma cried. Regaining her balance almost immediately, she spun and bounded after him.

Gabriel dashed after her.

The witch twisted as he ran, aiming his wand at her.

Another spear? The narrow aisle meant skewing it would only hit her with shrapnel. Gabriel knew he'd have to get her bodily out of the way instead.

"Emma, look out!" Not even bothering to hide his wand, he used it to wave something off a bottom shelf in front of her to trip her—just as the enemy witch released the spell.

Emma stumbled over the item—a thousand dollar tablet—and went to one knee as a huge gust of wind blew over her.

Gabriel had time to think *Thank the stars, that would have flattened her* before the wind plowed into him, so forceful it lifted him into the air.

An instant later he landed on his tailbone with an impact that rang pain up his spine.

Emma was stumbling up. Still first in the witch's line of fire.

Shunting aside his pain with a facility born of a hundred mock duels. Gabriel scrambled to his feet, readying his magic. He was screwed if she found out he was a witch, but better that than her suffering injury or worse.

But the other witch reached the end of the aisle, turned the corner, and disappeared.

Gabriel let go of his power, his ready magic evaporating, and started toward her.

She wavered on her feet, nose up. He realized she was testing the air. Then she turned and limped toward him. "He's gone."

He was outraged that the enemy witch had tried to hurt Emma. But seeing her limp...he'd done that, by tripping her.

Furious with himself, he swore. "That was a fucking disaster."

He was yelling at himself, but her shoulders sagged.

"Yes. The bait phone is gone. I tried to save it..."

"Oh, Emma." He strode to her, immediately contrite. "I know. You were wonderful." He stopped just short of gathering her in his arms. "Are you okay?"

Her big eyes rose to him, glossy. She released a relieved-sounding breath. "I'm fine. I thought you were yelling at me."

"No. Never." He did touch her then, because he had to, a light clasp on her slim shoulder.

She searched his eyes. A tremulous smile curved her lips, and he felt like howling in triumph.

Then she sighed. "But now we're back to square one." She bit her lip. "I mean you are. I thought I could help, but..."

She trailed off, her expression so sad and forlorn that he thought, *ah, hell*, and gathered her into his arms anyway. He only allowed himself a brief hug, trying very, very hard not to feel how soft and right she felt. He might be able to disguise his scent of desire, but no way he'd be able to hide the big ol' how-ya-doin' in his pants, not pressed together like this, rubbing almost intimately...his groin wrenched with desire and he sprang back, releasing her.

"It's *we*," he said. "We're not done yet. Come on." He started toward the back.

She trotted after him. "Where are we going?"

"My office."

"You put a tracer on the phone?" Her tone was admiring.

Normally he wasn't vain or someone who needed attention, but coming from her, that made him puff up.

"Two. One obvious, one hidden."

As he let them into his office, she said, "So, um. Are you really mad at me for interfering in your ambush?"

He shook his head. "I told you to go home because I was worried. That thief...he's dangerous. Did you see how he was both masked and gloved? And he had some kind of air-cannon weapon."

He sat down in front of his computer and brought up an app he'd written that displayed a map of the city and connected with his psychic eyes. As the screen refreshed, he surreptitiously touched a talisman on his belt. The talisman was linked to the tracker spell on the fake phone and was keyed to show the location on the map app.

Emma shivered as if she'd felt even the small bit of magic the talisman released. She was something. He really wanted to get to know her better. If only he could tell her he was a witch. He wished like buttered hell he'd never heard of the Witch's Council taboo.

A yellow dot appeared on a map of the city, heading rapidly east...and suddenly winked out.

"What does that mean?" Emma breathed.

It meant the witch had somehow countered or blinded his psychic eyes. "The thief found—and neutralized—both my tracers. Scrambled eggs and damn. Now how will we catch him?"

While in one way it was good the witch hadn't been royalty—there'd have been more power flung around and Emma might have gotten hurt—in another, it was very bad.

The number of royals was small, and Gabriel knew most of them. He'd have had at least a chance of identifying the thief.

Masked and gloved, the pool of potentials in the thousands? No way.

The only thing Gabriel could say for sure was the thief wasn't Emma or himself.

Although—terrifying thought—there was a real possibility the witch knew Gabriel was a mage, too. Even though he took great care to hide his magic and power, he hadn't always been so discreet.

Right now, the thief held all the cards.

* * *

*"Scrambled eggs and damn. Now how will we catch him?"*

Emma stood beside Dr. Light, her tummy shimmying from his nearness, his heat, size, and male beauty, and suddenly realized she knew the answer to that question.

*How will we catch him? I smelled him. I can identify him because* I know his scent.

The sheer joy rushing through her at the thought, *I can help Gabriel Light*, the giddy, dizzy need to help him, threw her.

She'd smelled rancid beef that first day here, in the office, but hadn't thought anything more of it. Then she'd sensed it at the crime scene, but passed it off as someone's lunch.

But tonight, she smelled spoiled meat in the air the witch had whipped up. It was all too apparent the smell belonged to the thief.

And since she'd also smelled it when Omniss had gotten her arrested...

She opened her mouth to name him.

Another thought hit her. She slowly closed her lips and played it out in her mind.

*"Dr. Light, I can name the thief. It's Mr. Omniss."*

*"How do you know?"*

What could she say to that? Anything she named, he'd be able to verify.

*"I saw a unique ring."*

*"I don't see any ring."*

*"I heard a pattern in his voice."*

*"I heard his voice too. No way anyone could tell that rasp was Omniss."*

*"I smelled him..."*

*"I don't smell anything. How can you?"*

No, the only way they could arrest Omniss was if Dr. Light took her on faith.

He'd never do that. Even her own family didn't just take her word for anything. How could a man she just met?

She wrapped her arms around herself—and felt the comforting weight of her new emergency bracelet.

She sighed. Since her father died and the Bloodfang debacle, she'd felt so alone. Then she'd waited with Dr. Light. Talked with him. Laughed with him.

Put on his bracelet.

*Tell him. Tell him Omniss is the thief.*

*He won't believe me. Not without proof.*

Her arms loosened and fell. And there was that bracelet, rolling down her wrist. A commitment to help her. *His* commitment.

Of all the people she knew, Dr. Light was the only one who might actually take her at her word.

If she trusted him.

It scared her. But she had to try. *I know you don't have any reason to believe me, but I'm asking you to. I know the thief is Omniss.*

She opened her mouth again to tell him.

A pounding started at the door.

"Gabriel Light," a man shouted. "Your security is worthless."

Emma exchanged a shocked glance with Dr. Light.

It was Omniss.

# Chapter Thirteen

"Gabriel Light," Omniss shouted. "Open up, now!"

Dr. Light shoved the chair back with an angry jerk, rose, and strode to the door.

*Omniss is here.* Emma flushed cold with doubt. Was she wrong? Was he not the thief?

Or was he *returning to the scene of the crime*?

She shifted her weight to her toes. "Dr. Light," she whispered urgently. "I have something to tell you. The thief is..."

Unlocking the door, he turned to her.

The door burst open and Omniss stalked triumphantly through...a scent of spoiled meat wafting before him.

Emma did the only thing she could. She met Dr. Light's gaze and nodded significantly toward the insurance adjuster.

Dr. Light frowned. Then his eyes widened slightly. He glanced at Omniss, his eyes returning immediately to hers, one brow quirked in a, *"No."*

Just to be sure, she inhaled. Definitely a mix of testosterone and rancid beef radiating from the insurance adjuster.

She nodded at Dr. Light. *"Yes."*

Dr. Light's gaze turned to Omniss and narrowed.

*He believes me.* Her whole being expanded with surprise and gratitude.

"It's pathetically easy to get in after hours," Omniss was saying. "I hid here tonight to prove it. Your supervisor locked up, never noticing I was here. Alone in the store, I could've stolen anything. I'm denying the original insurance claim, Light. And it's *your fault.*" He almost chortled it.

"Anybody ever tell you gloating is unattractive?" Dr. Light drawled, sauntering nearer to the man.

Panic flared in Emma's breast. Omniss was a witch. If Dr. Light tried to take him down, he might get hurt.

She gauged their positions. Omniss stood in front of Dr. Light's desk. She and Dr. Light made a V with the witch at the bottom. Emma was maybe two steps away, Dr. Light maybe three, but with Gabriel Light's long legs, probably two steps for him.

"You can, of course, appeal my decision," Omniss was saying. "Even if the fools at the home office overturn my decision, it'll take them months and months to work the claim through the system. Even years."

Emma could surprise Omniss, jump on his back and take him down, if Dr. Light distracted the witch.

Yes, Omniss was a witch, but she was an iota wolf. Though mostly small and weak compared to alphas and betas, she was still stronger than a human, and if she could catch him before he could use his magic, she was stronger than a witch.

All she had to do was surprise him.

All Dr. Light had to do was distract him.

The more she thought about it, the more she liked it. Besides taking Omniss down, Dr. Light wouldn't try to be the hero if he was busy distracting the witch.

She caught Dr. Light's eye. Mouthed, *"Distract him."* She made tiny gestures with her hand as if she was throwing a pebble into the corner of the room.

Dr. Light's eyes widened slightly. The smallest of nods.

"So if I were you, Gabriel Light," Omniss laughed, "I'd just take my lumps."

She held up a hand, turning slightly so that Omniss didn't see it. Three fingers.

Two fingers. One.

# Chapter Fourteen

Gabriel decided Emma was brilliant, so brilliant that he loved her.

She not only had identified Omniss as their thief, she realized he was a witch, and therefore dangerous.

Gabriel knew what she was planning. She wanted him to distract Omniss so she could attack the witch by surprise. And, if Gabriel were a normal man, that might even be the best plan for success.

But Gabriel was no normal man—he was a battle mage. As Emma folded down fingers, counting off, he took a step toward his desk.

Omniss saw him coming and frowned.

Gabriel reached deliberately toward his half-eaten dinner, bagel sitting in its paper wrap, open coffee cold beside it. As if he'd been unnerved enough by the man's threats to need to either comfort eat or clean.

Emma folded the last finger down.

Gabriel pretended to stumble into his desk. The cup of coffee knocked hard, splashing liquid up and out—and onto Omniss.

*Gotcha.*

As the other witch sputtered and slapped at his shirt, Gabriel said, "Sorry. That'll stain. Let me help."

Emma, beyond Omniss, flashed Gabriel a big smile. She thought this was his distraction.

*But wait*, he thought. *There's more.*

He put the flat of his hand to Omniss's chest. The man was an air witch, but as a wizard prince, Gabriel could use any element to augment his magic.

Emma leaped.

The instant they were both distracted, Gabriel touched his free hand to a talisman on his belt.

The talisman held a calming spell. He used it for customers who were so furious they couldn't do anything but shout, calming them enough that he could discover what their issue was to solve it. But it normally sent its calming vibes through the air, and an air mage could neutralize its effect.

Through water though, the thing was unstoppable.

Gabriel slammed the spell through his body and pumped it through his hand into Omniss's wet chest.

Omniss shuddered, the Calm spell penetrating deeply. His eyes rolled back in his head just as Emma hit him from behind. Gabriel danced back and let her carry the man to the floor.

"Nicely done," he said.

She wrestled Omniss's wrists behind him, not getting at first that the man was asleep. "We need to tie him up. A gag would help, too."

"Right. I've got zip ties that will do for wrist restraint for now." He went to his supply cabinet and grabbed a couple, marveling again at her quick thinking. Most witches needed their mouths and hands to cast spells or activate talismans. If Omniss had been awake, tying his hands and gagging him would be ninety-nine-percent proof against him casting spells.

When he came around the desk, she'd turned Omniss onto his back and was peeling up his eyelids one at a time. "He's unconscious. But I don't think he has a concussion or stroke."

"Strange," Gabriel said. "You didn't hit him hard enough to hurt him. Maybe he fell on something."

He'd said it to reassure her that she wasn't the cause, but he could see her quick brain pick up on it. Could see her consider the possibility that the witch had a hidden calming talisman, and when he fell, he'd activated it.

Close enough.

Gabriel zip-tied the man's wrists together. He used the act, bending close, to cover activating another talisman—a truth talisman. When Omniss woke, they'd get his confession.

The man's lids soon fluttered open.

Emma edged closer. Helping Omniss sit up, Gabriel could see she was readying herself to stop the witch from chanting a spell or snapping out a talisman activation command.

But Omniss only sat there, body wavering a bit woozily.

"Why?" Gabriel said. "Why'd you steal the Wrap-phone?"

Omniss turned a blank stare at him. "Stupid."

"Me?"

"Stupid question. Stupid marks. Too easy."

Gabriel touched another talisman under his vest, a wake-up. "You stole the phone because it was easy?"

The witch blinked, and lucidity returned to his eyes. He sneered, "Not just the phone. Jewelry, art, tech. The company insures it—putting the security details in the policy write-up."

His eyes widened, and his jaw snapped shut. He'd realized he'd been hit with a truth spell.

Wouldn't do him any good, though. Gabriel said, "You mean you skim insurance policies looking for small, high-end stuff that you can steal and sell?"

Omniss's jaw shuddered as he tried to keep silent. But he croaked, "For millions. Too easy. Even better, I go in afterward to do the investigation. Any mistakes, I can cover 'em up. Befuddle the police. Pin the blame." Falling on Emma, his gaze momentarily blazed.

Then that angry gaze came to Gabriel. "You." He shook his head. "Gabriel Light, so smart. So powerful. I talked to some people, suggested they ship the prototype early, so you couldn't put a physic...phsickick...damn."

Gabriel's breath stopped, waiting for the words *"So you couldn't put a psychic eye on it."* Words that would reveal Gabriel was a witch, too.

But Omniss only finished, "So you couldn't bug it."

He let out a relieved sigh. His secret was still safe. "Well, you nearly fooled us. We thought because the security cable wasn't cut, that it was an inside job. But you used some sort of tech to shake it open." He knew the shaking was air magic, but the question would hopefully misdirect Emma and reinforce him being mundane.

Lightly touching the Calm talisman again—it had a few more times before it would need recharging—he sent the other witch back to sleep. "Huh," he said. "Must be narcoleptic."

As he hoped, Emma rose, dusting off her hands. "Well, I'm glad we have proof it isn't me. I hope the police believe us when they come to take Mr. Omniss away. Um, as long as he's sleeping, I think I'm going to go use the restroom."

"Good idea. I'll stay here."

He knew where she was really going—someplace private to call the Witch's Council. They were the only people equipped to incarcerate a witch, but she wouldn't think Gabriel would know about it.

In the meantime, he called Carol, told her they'd caught the thief and asked her to come in. Her being there would force the Council Enforcers, when they arrived, to pretend to be mundane police. From there, the charade would spin out, everybody treating everyone else as if they were mundane, all for Carol's sake.

His secret would be safe. More importantly, Emma would be safe.

He'd have to give Carol a bonus for it. She wouldn't know why, but that didn't matter.

* * *

The next morning, Emma was facing product in the entertainment aisle when Dr. Light arrived.

She no longer even had to turn to see him stride into the store proper. She could feel his big, comforting presence.

"Everyone, gather 'round." Carrying a full plastic shopping bag, he hopped up onto the platform where he'd spoken that first day. "Mr. Crandall. If you'd come here, please." He waved at Brant.

The gangly teen loped eagerly toward the platform, leaping up like a colt—bashing straight into Dr. Light. Only the man's enormous strength kept them both from going down.

Then Gabriel Light's star-shot sea-blue eyes turned toward her. "Ms. Singer. If you'd join me on the stage."

Her heart began to thump. Hesitantly, she approached.

"Come on, Emma." Dr. Light gave her an encouraging smile. "If you can face Omniss, you can face this." He reached toward her.

Automatically, she put her hand in his. His palm engulfed her hand, the warmth and masculine power sending tremors shivering all the way to her belly. With a simple tug, he brought her flying onto the platform. Her belly swooped at the casual display of strength. Shockwaves of desire hit her sex, and her own scent turned distinctly musky. Her face heated. At least she knew a human Gabriel Light couldn't smell it.

"Today I want to present two people who have trained long and hard and have achieved the highest honor we can bestow." He reached into the bag and drew out a folded stack in Choice Buy blue, a small rectangle lying on top of it. "Ms. Singer." He handed the stack to her.

She trembled, this time with hope. As he called Brant's name and dug in the bag a second time, she looked at the rectangle.

It read "Emma Singer—Techie Titan."

Her eyes itched with tears. She shook out the material to reveal an official Choice Buy polo shirt.

As Dr. Light handed Brant his permanent shirt, badge, and emergency bracelet, he spoke to them both, but his gaze was on her.

"You're part of the team, now. We will always be here to support you. If you have problems, we're here to work things through with you. If you have joy, we're here to share it and make it even more special. Mr. Crandall, Ms. Singer—welcome to my team."

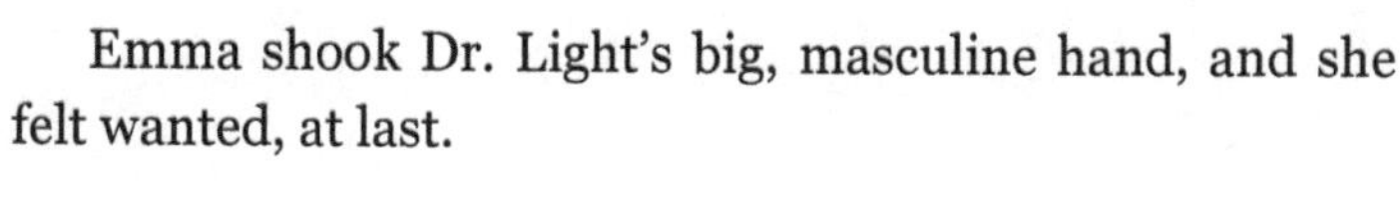

Emma shook Dr. Light's big, masculine hand, and she felt wanted, at last.

Continue reading for excerpts from Prophecy Mates (Pull of the Moon Book 1) and Mind Mates (Pull of the Moon Book 4).

# About Mary Hughes

Mary Hughes (written Hug-he's but possibly pronounced throat warbler mangrove) writes smart and sassy stories of action and love.

She's a bona fide computer geek and performing flutist. (And piccolo, but we don't talk about that.) When this USA Today Bestselling Author isn't busy finding the missing </> tag or blowing her lungs out, she's on the couch reading or binging on The Flash, Elementary, NCIS, or Wynonna Earp...and petting the cats that inevitably end up on her lap.

Mary's online and would love to hear from you!
Newsletter http://www.maryhughesbooks.com/Newsletter.html
Facebook http://www.facebook.com/MaryHughesAuthor
Twitter http://www.twitter.com/MaryHughesBooks
Instagram https://www.instagram.com/maryhughesbooks
BookBub https://www.bookbub.com/authors/mary-hughes
Goodreads
http://www.goodreads.com/author/show/279140.Mary_Hughes
Website http://www.maryhughesbooks.com/
Blog http://maryhughesbooks.blogspot.com/

*The masks are coming off.*

**Prophecy Mates**



Pull of the Moon Book 1

Daniel Light is a powerful wizard prince on the hunt for a dangerous prophecy—only to find it's in the hands of Zoe Blackwood, the woman he'd adored, and who'd firmly friend-zoned him, when he was a gangly teen. Daniel can get his hands on the prophecy by seducing Zoe at a masked ball, settling accounts with her. Yet he finds he wants to woo her.

Wolf shifter Zoe throws a classy, grand masked ball as her last chance at romance before her wolf forces her to mate. She remembers Daniel as that rich, awkward boy she could always count on yet never really noticed. When he shocks her by showing up at her ball, he's still rich but not awkward at all, and she notices his deadly grace plenty. But can she still count on him?

Then an evil fire wizard crashes the party, eager to get his hot hands on Zoe—and her prize, an ancient parchment. She's horrified to discover both men are really after the parchment for its hidden prophecy—and she's caught in the crosshairs.

Over the top, fun and action-packed, short and hot! If you like your heroes staunch, powerful, and faithful, this is the one for you!

Enjoy the following first chapter from *Prophecy Mates*:

“Damn it.” Wizard prince Daniel Light zipped his Ferrari along Lincoln Memorial Drive, the lapping waters of Lake Michigan to his right—along with a solid line of parked cars. He spoke into his wireless hands-free, connected to the phone in his tuxedo jacket pocket. “Not a single open space between here and the moon. And me, late for the party.”

“Isn’t being late for a party a good thing?” Cousin Sophia said in his ear, her voice like honeyed whiskey.

“Not with that prophecy ticking.”

An old parchment bearing a nasty prophecy was tonight’s prize for romancing a beautiful woman—a masked-ball Bachelorette contest. Daniel took the event as a challenge, to see how far he’d come from his painful high school days.

Seemed the real challenge was finding parking.

“Double damn with a side of blast. I don’t have time for this.” He spun a U-turn and slid his car into a tow-away spot smack in front of a waterfall of stairs, the back entrance to a mansion villa high atop a bluff. “I’m here.”

“You found legal parking?” Sophia asked.

“I found parking. Legal is more of a movable concept. If that prophecy is as dangerous as we think it is, I might need a quick getaway.”

“Does telling yourself that help you sleep at night?” A smile was in her tone.

He laughed. “Oh believe me, I do whatever it takes to get the job done.”

The clop-clop of horse’s hooves along asphalt caught his attention.

"Hell's bells. Hold on." He glanced into his rearview mirror. A large, dark shadow moved between pools of light. He twisted in his seat to see better.

Bearing down on him was a mounted police officer, her mouth pressed in a tight line.

"What's wrong?" Sophia's voice was breathy and anxious in his ear. "Is it a mugger? A *demon?*"

"A cop."

"Oh." A self-conscious laugh. "That's almost worse, considering your 'movable' legality. I hope it's not a bad omen."

"You wound me. When has my luck been anything but great?"

"In high school—"

"Yes, yes, all right. But I've come a long way from my dork prince days."

These days, no one could play the game of love better than Daniel. He'd honed his body, gathered a fortune, and polished his social graces until most every woman loved him.

All to shield his fragile heart.

Daniel sprang out of the Ferrari in his immaculate black tux. "Good evening, officer."

"Sir, you can't park here." The woman reined in, gaze hard.

"I'm so sorry. I'm late for an important event." He stepped into a streetlamp's golden glow, tilted his head at just the right angle for the light to kiss his blond hair, and gave her his best smile, enhanced with a twinkle of magic.

Her eyes widened. She blinked a few times, and there was a creak as she adjusted her seat as if her saddle was too hot. "Sir, this is a tow-away zone."

"I'm sorry," He said again, reaching reached a hand toward her horse. "May I?"

When she nodded, he ran his palm along its sleek neck. The gelding nickered.

"A fine Morgan," he said.

Her expression softened. "You know horses?"

"I have a way with animals." He continued to stroke. "Officer, I know I shouldn't ask this, but I'm late, and it's extremely important I get to this event." He raised his eyes to meet hers, not a soulgaze, but he was a wizard prince, and his power gave his eyes a certain charisma. "Just this once?"

"Well..." She blushed. "Just this once."

"Thank you. You won't regret it." As he mounted the first of several long flights of stairs up the bluff , he ticked a mental note to discover what charities her department supported. He'd make some sizeable contributions in thanks. Anonymous, of course.

"Still stunning them with your good looks, Cuz?" Sophia's amusement sparkled in her voice.

"If you've got it, use it, or lose it."

She *tsked*. "You're mixing your metaphors again."

"Metaphors are like alcohol. They should be mixed early and often. In this case, though, a little magical suggestion helped."

"That's cheating."

"Enhancing,' he countered.

"Cheating," she said firmly. "I think I miss the old, serious Daniel. Witchkind—hell, magic itself—is at stake if we don't find Jean-Dion d'Avignon's lost prophecy...and you're playing at a party."

"Halloween masked ball, actually." He crested onto a terrace. Reaching into his tuxedo's jetted side pocket, he pulled out a Zorro-style black mask then tied it on as he crossed the terrace. “This is work, not play. The prophecy is here.”

She sucked in a breath. “At a ball?”

“Tonight’s prize is a parchment.” He bounded lightly up another angle-bracket stairs, one of a pair that scissored to the top. “The parchment bears the Avignon Quatrain.”

“You know this, how?”

“How else? Arianna told me. It’s quite convenient to have a family seer.”

“Convenient.” Sophia sniffed. “You obviously never played poker with her. How do you win this prize parchment?”

“By tenderly, passionately wooing a woman.” He reached the upper terrace, threading his way through sumptuous sculpture, topiary, and a swarm of women in silky gowns and men in severe suits.

He continued, “At midnight, the hostess, the Queen of Hearts, is offering a ‘valuable antiquity’ as a prize. She doesn’t know how valuable.”

Sophia whistled. “But it’s a *masked* ball. How will you know which woman to woo?”

He joined the stream of glitterati entering the villa. “Considering the stakes—I’ll make love to them all.”

“That’ll try your stamina.”

“But ah, such a trial.”

She laughed then said goodbye. He ended the call and slipped the earbud into his tuxedo’s breast pocket.

The ballroom doors were closed. He glided through the waiting throng. Beautiful women surrounded him, smiling and nodding. As he considered which he’d woo first, his body tingled pleasantly in anticipation.

Memory of rich mahogany hair, gorgeous curves, and a generous smile stopped him. His high school crush, who'd never noticed him—a woman he'd never forgotten.

Zoe Blackwood.

He sighed. Maybe he'd wait until the doors opened to start wooing.

* * *

"Dammit, Dorine, how can I have forgotten to turn on the champagne fountain?" Zoe Singer Blackwood, motorcycle-dealership owner and secret wolf shifter, sailed through the back of the ballroom, dodging wait staff tending the laden buffet tables.

"I'm sorry, Ms. Blackwood." Her stalwart event planner, clutching her ever-present clipboard, scurried to keep pace. "That was my job."

"Your job—my responsibility. Granted, I'm not expecting much, romance-wise, from tonight's crop of bachelors, but I'd like to give them a chance. Speaking of..." Zoe caught sight of her nearly naked breasts in the wall of gold-encrusted mirrors. "Your taste in decorations is impeccable. Your advice in clothes, not so much." She tugged up the spangled bodice of her little black strapless number. On the model, it was cut to showcase feminine assets; on Zoe's lush figure, it was a rubber band with a ruffle. "I want to make romance, not a porno."

"Still getting dressed?" The deep voice in her earbud was amused. "Hasn't your shindig already started?"

"Bite me, Noah." She adjusted the earpiece, trying not to tangle it in the elastic holding her thin black domino mask in place. The phone itself was in her purse in one of the prep rooms a hundred or so feet away. For the first time, she wished the earbud's range wasn't quite so far.

"I can't bite you," he said reasonably. "We're related."

"Just because you're going to be my alpha one day doesn't mean you can be a jackass."

Zoe headed for the center table dominated by a three-tiered crystal fountain, currently dark and silent. She crawled under a white-linen tablecloth to flip the fountain's rocker switch. The burble of liquid started, then splashed as champagne cascaded.

As she backed out, she found Dorine staring at her backside, embarrassment clear on her maskless face.

"You might be right about the dress," the planner said. "Um, cute panties."

"Thanks," Zoe said dryly. She stood, brushed hands and knees, adjusted her mask, then tugged down her hem. Her breasts bobbled dangerously, and she sighed. "How's the rest of that checklist?"

"Good." Dorine's red face ebbed as she ticked efficiently on her clipboard. "Decorations complete, food laid out, bartenders here, and bars fully stocked. Orchestra assembling. We're ready." Her gaze flicked to Zoe's bosom, and her cheeks practically went *bomf*. "Except for you, that is."

Zoe caught sight of herself in the mirrors. Her nipple waved hi. She tugged the dress up—which bared her stocking tops. She shook her head and gave up. "This party isn't about me. This is for all the women like me who've had enough of pawing guys. Women who want romance—or at least a few candles and cuddles before the mauling."

"Candles and cuddles. Yes, Ms. Blackwood. I'll go check on the greeters."

"Wait. I meant to say thanks. For everything. The place looks enchanting."

"You're welcome." With a small, pleased smile, Dorine left.

Zoe's gaze swept the room. Red streamers, sweet-smelling flowers, champagne, and choice tidbits of shrimp, cheese, and *petits fours*.

If guys couldn't get their romance on with all this, they weren't trying.

"Why a ball?" Noah asked in her ear.

Because she'd had one glimpse of romance, in high school. One rich, classy, untouchable boy amid all the under-the-bleacher gropes. He'd shown her what real love was, the kind that didn't have sex strings attached. That sweet-down-to-her-toes feeling was unforgettable. She was trying to recreate it with a rich, classy ball.

But she didn't know how to say all that in a way Noah would understand.

"Didn't you call to give me a pack update?" she asked, instead.

"Avoiding the question? All right."

As he bullet-pointed the latest atrocities by their idiot alpha Scauth, she sailed around the ballroom, double-checking everything.

When Noah finished, he said, "I wish you were here."

"Matinsfield needs my income more than it needs my jaws and paws. And with you there, the money I make with the motorcycle store is actually getting to hungry mothers and pups. Before, it only made it as far as Scauth's liquor cabinet."

"Except for the cash you spend on fancy parties."

"Just this one," she defended. "Doing sophisticated and romantic isn't cheap, you know. I've got an orchestra with real strings and everything."

"All to find a date? Wasn't MatchShift.com good enough?"

"Noah, I'm thirty-nine. You know what that means. When I hit forty, my wolf will *force* me to take a mate."

"You've given up finding Mr. Right?"

"Or even Mr. Good Enough. In one year, I'll get Mr. Pup Daddy whether I want him or not." She shuddered at the thought. "Before I do, you bet I'm gonna get me Some Enchanted Evenings."

"Zoe, you're a shifter. You have your pick of men."

"Sure, my wolf gets me plenty of sex, but romance? I've seen too many beds—and couches and tabletops. My human knows there's more. Roses and poetry and walks on moonlit beaches."

"Lake Michigan? More like pebbles in your paws." The humor dropped from his tone. "Throwing a ball with nice clothes and live music isn't going to stop men from being men."

"Exactly why I need tonight." Once she was mated, she and her mate would be pawing each other constantly. Tonight, before it was too late, she'd get a reminder of what romance felt like.

She desperately needed to find and hang onto that feeling. So that, in the gritty beach of constant animal sex, she'd recognize the few grains of true love.

"I have a cunning plan to encourage romance."

"Saltpeter in the mashed potatoes?" Noah suggested. "Meat-cleaver vasectomy?"

"Ha. No, I'm offering a prize. My family heirloom, the Singer Parchment." She turned toward the crown of the evening, resting in its glass case at the foot of the golden, bubbling champagne fountain. "Beautiful, full-color, illuminated capital letters. Authentic parchment and ink from the late House of Valois period in France. My father had it validated."

There it was, safe in its locked display.

With the key...still in the lock.

She straightened abruptly and shouted, "Dorine. Key!"

"Ow." Noah's voice was pained.

"Sorry. Damn my paws, where is that planner?"

Dorine was nowhere to be seen. Zoe flew to the case, plucked out the small key, and dropped it in her décolletage. "Everything would be ruined if the prize was stolen."

"The Valuable Heirloom Parchment?" His tone was dry.

"Laugh all you want, but it'll work. The prize will go to whoever romances me the best—and here's the best part. Since we're *all* masked, the guys won't know who I am. The men *can't* be men. They'll have to court all the women here. Cool, or what?"

"Cool," Noah admitted. "But why an antique for a prize? Wouldn't the guys respond better to stadium tickets or free beer?"

"Seriously? My kind of 'man' would respond better to chasing rabbits in the woods. But for sweet, romantic men, antiquities and art are a better lure."

"Considering the males you normally date, you know this, how?"

"I met a nice boy, once," she tried to explain. "A rich boy. He told me about a lavish, romantic ball his parents threw. White tie, orchestra, parchment party favors, the works— including a genuine antique door prize. Absolutely magical."

Trying to recreate that magic, she'd sent out two hundred invites to the city's most sophisticated, eligible singles. Then, because all this only for her would be selfish, she'd personally invited the women from the local shelter where she volunteered. She wanted to give them the same chance she'd had—a glimpse of something better. To know, at least once, what it was like to be wooed by a truly attentive man.

"That parchment has been in your family for generations. I'm surprised your mother agreed to it."

"It's mine," Zoe said quickly. "Dad's family. Mom was just holding it for me."

"Meaning what?"

She hesitated, then lowered her voice. "Mom doesn't actually know."

"She *what?*"

Zoe winced. "Noah, please don't blab to her. I kind of had to. You know that round little woman who runs the weird bookstore in Matinsfield, with all the crystals and stuff?"

"Only by reputation."

"Old lady Blue is a fortuneteller on the side. I bumped into her on my last visit home, and she told me I needed to get rid of the parchment *or else*."

Actually, Blue said if Zoe didn't get rid of the parchment—on Halloween, no less—an evil witch would come and probably kill whoever possessed it. Shifters couldn't identify witches on sight, but they did know about them. Evil witches were nasty, nightmare stuff. Zoe couldn't leave the parchment with her mom.

"That doesn't sound good." All the playfulness left Noah's deep voice. "Or else what?"

"Oh, it's probably nothing. You know seers. Gotta pump up the doom." Zoe peered into the display case, expecting to see the usual four words, HEART, MIND, SOUL, and KEY.

Letters blazed across the top, *Give this to the Light, Zoe*—then poofed the instant she'd read them, throwing her heart into her throat.

She gasped.

"Zoe? *What's* going on?" Noah's growl wasn't the cousin requesting information, it was the alpha-to-be demanding it. So alpha it made her human wince, and her wolf whine.

But if she told him, he'd be on the next bus into town, despite pack women up north needing him more. How could she dodge this silver bullet?

"Sorry, time to open the doors. Gotta go!" Zoe clicked off and tucked the small earpiece next to the key in her cleavage—plenty of room, with her measurements.

Then, because she didn't want to be a liar, she signaled the greeters to open the door.

Tuxedoed men and women in dresses from long and floaty to short and sassy flowed into the room. Zoe smoothed hands along hips, her stomach churning with both nerves and excitement. It surprised her; her wolf wasn't usually jumpy. A good run would take care of that, but she couldn't leave her guests.

She was double-checking the cheese table when she heard a cry.

"Get your paws off me!"

Female, high, stressed. Behind her.

Zoe's wolf snapped her around. Her gaze zoomed in on a woman in a simple, silver lamé sheathe at a nearby hors d'oeuvre table. A woman from the shelter.

A would-be Romeo in a marquess's sash with enough medals to be its own platoon had backed the woman into the table.

"Stop it." The woman slapped at the marquessy guy, fending off his hands, her flailing arms stirring a storm of rose petals and heart-shaped confetti. "I said *stop*."

"You like it, baby." He grabbed private lamé and puckered up.

Damn it, this was exactly what the woman didn't need. Zoe ran in, seized the guy's wrist and yanked it like the string of a yo-yo.

He spun away from the woman, straight into Zoe's glare.

"Romance, asshole." To make sure he got the message, she put a little wolf into it.

His mask-on-a-stick dropped to swing from its ribbon. The surprised O of his mouth was almost funny.

Then she breathed in, and the alcohol fumes surrounding him stung her nose like a liquor smog. The guy was practically one hundred proof. Either he'd loaded up before coming or he'd been bathing in the champagne fountain. "On second thought, you're done." She marched him toward the door, trying not to breathe too deeply.

"Wh-why? I was romancing her."

"Romance does *not* mean feeling a woman up like a Japanese body pillow." She shoved him toward the greeters. She'd have applied boot to butt if her dress hadn't been in danger of doing a window-shade roll up.

Twist her tail, this evening was *not* starting well. Palming her nape, she returned to the back of the room.

A dark-haired man bent over the parchment case, caressing it as if studying it—or trying to make out with it, she wasn't sure. Still, if he was interested in the parchment that meant he was classy, right?

Zoe took a deep breath. Okay. Time to find romance. Donning her best Mona Lisa smile, she sidled up behind him and pitched her voice low and sultry, just short of *Lookin' for a good time, sailor?* "Hello."

He jerked around as if annoyed.

A brutal cowl of ripped, stitched leather, partially masking an equally brutal face, confronted her. Small, mismatched holes showed piggy eyes. His gaze dropped precipitously, catching on her breasts and heating as lustfully as if he had X-ray vision.

She had to work to keep her smile in place. "I'm Lady Mystery."

"Not much mystery." He pointed at her bared cleavage—like she was in danger of missing his clever wit. His voice was as rough as a chainsaw. Slowly, his gaze rose, not quite reaching the level of hers, and his lips curled in a smile made of creamed smarm. He held out his hand. "Zeus."

The name of the top-of-the-food-chain Greek god. No lack of ego there.

Still, that flirting wasn't going to do itself. She shook his hand briefly. Tried to let go, but he tightened his grip and used it to tug her closer. Her belly fluttered uneasily. He reeked of testosterone, the kind filled with anger and ambition. Her wolf's senses were preternaturally heightened but even a human would have smelled it.

"Let's you and me get to know each other, Lady Mystery." He rubbed a palm over her arm, not rough, but not entirely comfortable.

She gritted her teeth and told herself she was overreacting. *Flirt. Enjoy.* "Sure."

He put an arm around her shoulders. His fingers traipsed along her collarbone until they tickled. But then they took a walk on the wild side of her breastbone, spelunking down her cleavage.

Enough was enough. She cleared her throat to make some classy excuse to beat his head into the wall.

Before she could, a buzz at the door distracted her. She glanced up as the crowd parted.

A blond man glided in like a panther, stopped, and stood there, as tall and confident as if he owned the place. He was built like a true Greek god, inverted triangle torso on long, strong legs. His golden hair shone lustrous in the electric light. His strong features accented by a rakish black mask drew the eye of every female in the room.

* * *

After the ballroom doors opened, Daniel waited until the crowd had thinned to make a proper entrance.

He stepped into the ballroom with confidence. The space was lavishly decorated, an orchestra to one side. He gently flirted with a pair of blonde greeters.

Then the crowd parted.

A woman stood there. The rest of the room faded until bright light haloed her and only her.

Spring-green eyes shone against the black of her domino mask. Glossy hair rippled like a living mahogany waterfall. Her lush figure was banded provocatively in black glitter. She held herself with the sensuous grace, not of a dancer, but a lioness.

Daniel's heart leaped and began to pound. His blood heated until it almost boiled. He started toward her with a lion's hunting prowl.

As he neared, her scent hit him, a complex mixture of jasmine, saffron, and woman. That scent...

He knew her.

His breath caught. Pulse leaping, he took one last stuttering step toward her.

High school memories crowded him. Her lush body, her sweet smile, her kind soul...and the most erotic dreams a boy ever had. Or a man still had.

Zoe Blackwood.

* * *

Zoe peeled off Zeus' arm and moved from him as if he'd never existed.

The blond man's gaze swung to her—and stopped.

Instant connection sang between them. It rang in her ears, in her blood, so powerful and shocking it kicked the air out of her lungs.

The man started toward her, cutting through the crowd like a sleek ship.

Her breath returned in quick, excited puffs.

His scent hit her as he neared, catapulting her back in time to cheerleader sweaters and smoking blunts in the woods...and the burnt scent of an almost-failed chemistry class.

"Damn my paws," she muttered.

Daniel Light.

*Pretty little shifter, wizard prince—their taboo love could burn the barriers between worlds.*

**Mind Mates**
© 2016 Mary Hughes

Pull of the Moon Book 4

Shifter Emma Singer has more problems than she can shake her pretty wolf tail at. Her father has been executed, and her mother and brother plan to sell her to a pack alpha for his harem. Even the wicked little crush she has on her boss is doomed–why would six-and-a-half feet of hot, handsome, royal wizard want a boring, good-girl, iota shifter like her? Not to mention her only power is going berserker–that's a real relation-shipwreck!

Gabriel Light is a wizard prince who turned his back on his exceptional powers after he was accused of causing his parents' death. Now he pours his intellect into his tech business, and hides his naughty, forbidden lust for his pretty shifter clerk. But when his sister is imprisoned, and Emma is kidnapped, it's time for this alpha-geek wizard to decloak with all laser cannons blazing. Only one problem–with Emma at his side, how can he stay focused, with his inner wolf howling to have her?

Emma's father left behind a journal. When Gabriel and Emma accidentally release its hidden magic, they learn that together, they hold a key to power beyond imagining–if they can stay alive long enough to use it. But when Emma unleashes her berserker wolf on their enemies, can

Gabriel draw her back from the brink before she destroys everyone in her path?

*Warning: Contains a hot wizard prince panting to bring out a good-girl shifter's naughty side. Accidental voyeurism, deliberate orgasms, a jealous rival wizard, and fun with prophecy*

Enjoy the following first chapter from *Mind Mates*:

Swaying atop the three-story ladder, Emma Singer swallowed hard and forced herself to climb higher.

Her fingers curled tighter around the rungs as she neared the metal braces of the Choice Buy's exposed-structure ceiling. An Employee Appreciation Day banner drooped from her clenched hand.

"Damn. This good-girl shtick is getting old."

Wolf shifters, even iotas, weren't afraid of heights, but her stomach slid toward her legs the higher she got, maybe knowing something she didn't.

She glanced down and immediately wished she hadn't.

From the hushed, rarefied heights, her fellow Techie Titans looked like ants gathered around the home-theater setup, where their boss was installing a game. The huge flat-panel was reduced to postage-stamp size by her height.

Strangely, her six-foot-five boss looked just as imposing as usual.

"Hurry up, Emma." Brant the Blundering, the gangly teen who'd pulled down the streamer in the first place, called from the base of the ladder. He was built like a puppy who hadn't grown into his paws—and was as coordinated too.

Swallowing her vertigo, she stretched to refasten the crepe paper to a joist.

"More to the right." Brant waved an arm to demonstrate, hand like an oven mitt on a broomstick.

He hit the ladder and knocked it sideways.

Emma tottered, arms pinwheeling. The streamer fluttered away, waving mockingly in crepe paper's version of the finger.

*No good deed goes unpunished* flashed through her thoughts as she toppled off. The ladder rocked a few times before righting itself with a *kerchunk*.

It seemed an eternity for Emma to fall the three stories. Below, Brant's wide eyes followed her descent. She had time to wonder if there was a twelve-stepper for acute volunteeritis.

*Well. This is gonna hurt.*

"Emma!" In the nick of time her boss, Dr. Gabriel Light, swooped in, doing his usual hero thing.

He caught her.

She landed in his strong arms (no problem). They were tight around her (no problem). His scent, masculine and heady, filled her sudden sucked breath (still no problem, or not much of one).

Automatically she clung to his broad shoulders, hard muscles under her fingers, her inner wolf wagging its tail (starting to be a problem). Her fingers threaded into his silky hair (definitely trekking into problem territory). Her lips, a whisper from his chiseled jaw, his delectable earlobe, opened, her tongue aching to swipe a taste.

Red-alert problem.

"Emma, you're safe. Trust me." Behind his plain glasses, his lids lifted to her. His irises were a startling, star-shot blue-green, like the moon sparkling off a warm sea, making her want to dive in and do the breaststroke.

For all that he dressed like a junior college professor, the man was teeth-achingly beautiful.

She tried to swallow, but her tongue had swollen to fill her mouth and nothing happened. She tried again, managing to pant and gulp at the same time, swallowed wrong, and started coughing uncontrollably.

Dr. Light set her on her feet—by sliding her down his sleek, muscular, cotton-and-male-smelling chest, oh *yum*—and rubbed her between her shoulders to ease her.

His big, warm palm did ease her cough, but the breadth of his hand filled the entire area between her shoulder blades and made the rest of her clench with aching desire. Gabriel Light wasn't simply lead Techie Titan—he was their nerd king, and he was built like royalty.

The little iota wolf in Emma yipped happily.

But she, her human self, wasn't so pleased. Despite her interest in him, he'd never shown anything more than kindly concern. The last thing she wanted was to be a poor lovesick fool.

But he smelled so *good.*

"Are you all right?" Dr. Light, one arm clasped around her, slid a long, large finger under her chin. Tilting her head up, he gazed deep into her eyes. His own were sympathetic.

She stopped breathing at the oceans of tenderness in that gaze—fraternal tenderness, but so damned gorgeous.

Plus side, no breath meant her hacking cough stopped, long enough for her to wheeze with what air remained in her lungs, "I'm fine."

One corner of his mouth tipped up in a gentle semi-smile. "You always say that. 'I'm fine.' Whether you are or not. You're not a trainee anymore, Emma. It's okay not to be fine. You won't get fired. It's okay to admit you need help."

An iota wolf, admit to being vulnerable? Hell no, it wasn't okay. Her breath surged back in a rush. She was bottom of the pack, and worse, built like a kitten, tiny and cute to the point that she had to buy her clothes in the kids' section at WallyWorld and one of her nicknames was Piglet. She could never *ever* be caught out as needy and vulnerable, surrounded by apex predators all day.

She wasn't sure whether she meant her shifter pack or the six-foot-five walking sex bomb who was her boss.

*Human* boss, she reminded herself. Who didn't seem to have a *clue* she was interested in him.

"I'm *fine,*" she repeated through clenched teeth.

"Are you?" His gaze shifted to her mouth, and she stopped breathing again. "That's bad for your teeth, you know. Relax."

He eased the chiding words with a slide of his finger along her jaw, the rough whorls of the pad caressing her flesh. His touch raised tremors in her that shimmered down her throat, waking nipples and belly and wolf.

Oh, to grab him, hook a leg behind his, and take him down to the floor—with her underneath.

She was strong and tricky and might have tried it in private, except he moved like he'd studied martial arts and knew what to do. A warrior's grace hinted at an extremely muscular body lurking beneath his sweater vests and slouchy pants. She'd probably only embarrass herself.

Her wolf didn't seem to care. It was panting and lifting its tail, and her human wasn't far behind.

So naturally, when her eyes were big pools of do-me and she was spurting pheromones like a department store perfumery, her alpha wolf Bruiser prowled into the store.

* * *

*Bzz-bzzt.* A buzz like an angry hornet stung wizard prince Gabriel Light's ears the moment the predator slunk into the store.

*Cap'n Crunch me.* Gabriel had magically alarmed the door for just such an event, but why now, when he'd finally gotten a semi-innocent excuse to wrap his arms around this warm bundle of soft, sweet-smelling heaven?

Emma. It felt like he'd been dying to hold her forever. Now, with her in his arms, was the first time in months he could breathe.

But that buzzing alarm told him the approaching beast was male, a wolf shifter, and, from that level of sting, Emma's alpha. The beast was not going to appreciate seeing her in another man's arms.

She started trembling, no doubt in response to the alpha's rampant fight-club stench, a musk even Gabriel could smell. He tried to ease her tension with a joke.

"Hey, Emma. How many tickles does it take to make an octopus laugh?"

She skewered him with a disbelieving stare, icing his flesh. He'd blundered, she didn't understand he was trying to comfort her, *nobody gets my skewed sense of humor...* Then she gulped and said, "Eight? Like, um, eight legs?"

Immediately his world brightened. "Nope. Ten tickles. Get it? Tentacles?"

She managed a tiny laugh, tinkling bells to his ears, and her body relaxed slightly under his arms. "That was *such* a dad joke."

He loved that she, of all the people he knew, actually laughed at his jokes. He smiled into her eyes like a besotted fool.

Of course, that was when the he-wolf prowled into view.

Gabriel wondered how far he could get with the wolf by protesting his intentions were honorable. Probably not far. The creature was only barely in human form.

The wolfman was medium height but had a face like a dented shovel and a body like a trash compactor, his muscles-on-muscles popping in a stringy T-shirt that barely qualified past no-shirt-no-shoes-no-service.

Worse, with the hair sprouting everywhere, nose elongating like a snout, and lengthening canines, this alpha was dangerously pissed.

Hard to reason with a pissed-off wolf. They tended to bite first then ask questions...never.

Yet instead of releasing Emma, Gabriel's hand dropped from her clenched jaw to open protectively on her back.

"The fuck?" the wolfman snarled.

Something inside Gabriel snarled right back.

He throttled it. Whether his own masculine instincts or maybe he'd developed a wolf to complement Emma's, *down boy*. Diplomacy first. "This isn't what it seems—"

"I know." The he-wolf tapped his snout. "Good thing too, or you'd already have my fist in your face. Let her go. *Now*."

Briefly Gabriel clenched his eyes. The wolf didn't smell it, but Gabriel really reeked of desire. He'd magicked up a way to hide the odor because of the Witches' Council.

Witches tangling bed sheets with wolves was a huge taboo—punishable by anything up to and including the headsman's axe. He'd have risked the ultra-close shave, but the Council Enforcers usually hit the female with the worst of the punishment.

He couldn't stand the idea of one hair on Emma's head being harmed.

Trying to deescalate the situation, Gabriel loosened his arms around her. But he couldn't quite let her go. "Sorry, sir." He forced a smile and managed a creditable professionalese. "Store's closed. Private party."

"In the middle of the fuckin' day?"

"Yes, sir. A special recognition celebration." He had a small one every month, but this month they'd had record sales, so he closed the store early, locked the doors, and put on a real shindig. He wondered momentarily how the he-wolf had gotten in. Maybe with the caterers. "You'll have to leave."

"Not without her."

"Sir, what part of private eludes you?"

The wolf held up one ham hand and slowly curled his fingers. "What part of my fist eludes *you?* If I'm leaving, so is my cousin."

Probably not by DNA. "Cousin" was a common cover story for pack members living together, caring for each other, *getting naked together...* Gabriel's arms tightened around the pretty little shifter. The he-wolf growled in response. Gabriel would have to let go of her.

Soon.

At least the creature didn't know Gabriel was a witch. No one would, unless he was working active magic. If the wolfman *had* known, he would've attacked immediately. The Witches' Council's taboo meant most wolves had no use for witches, and some actively hated them.

*Let her go.*

Problem was, if he stepped away now the alpha would see Gabriel's intentions were no longer perfectly honorable.

Slouchy pants only covered so many inches of rock-hard hey-how-ya-doin'?

The wolf stalked nearer.

*Let her go.*

*Not yet.*

Hell and cornflakes, Gabriel had been constantly aroused, ever since Emma started working at his store two months ago. Her pretty face, pert body, and sparkling personality called to everything in him.

What nailed it was that she actually got his weird sense of humor.

The he-wolf prowled the edge of Gabriel's kill zone. Getting steamed.

Gabriel really needed to let Emma go.

But none of it seemed to matter squat, not Witches' Council headsman nor the hairy promise of death, not when his dreams had become reality at last, and he had her soft, curvy body in his arms.

"Dr. Light, it's okay." Emma's sweet voice snared his attention. "I know this, um, man."

She gazed up into his face so adoringly he fell into her big brown eyes, momentarily blotting the alpha shifter from his awareness.

Which was when the wolfman grabbed Emma's delicate arm in one hairy ham hand and yanked her out of Gabriel's embrace.

Yanked her so hard she stumbled.

Fury seized Gabriel. He grabbed the wolf's slab of a shoulder and shoved him back, popping Emma loose. Stalking after, Gabriel tore off his glasses to glare down at the he-wolf. Bad idea to challenge an alpha, but *this beast dared touch Emma.*

The wolfman's ears lengthened and definite fangs flashed. "What the fuck do you think you're doing?"

Gabriel ripped out, "*Nobody* manhandles a woman, or *any* being, in my...in our store." His jaw clenched against his slip of the tongue. At pains to blend in, he didn't advertise the fact that he owned this Choice Buy. Hell, head Techie Titan was bad enough. He'd taken great care to stay under both mundane and magical radars, to the point of wearing glasses he didn't need. Huffing a calming breath, he put said glasses back in place.

"That is my cousin, and I'm head of the family." The he-wolf's eyes narrowed, spitting fire. "You interferin' in family business?"

While the wolfman spoke, his hairy hand dipped behind his back—where a concealed gun or knife would be.

Damn it. Gabriel played the wimpy nerd to humans and potion geek to witches to avoid exactly this.

Mentally, he called up a shield spell. Violence was about to erupt.

"Enough!" Emma wedged her tiny self between them, shoulders back, chin up, and chest puffed like an irate cat's fur. "Bruiser—I mean Bruce. Leave Dr. Light alone."

Gabriel found himself a little surprised and a lot impressed. She was standing up to a wolf twice her size and her alpha to boot.

This was a totally new side to her. In the couple months she'd worked here, she'd only ever been diffident. Eager to please.

Always saying "I'm fine". He found himself even more intrigued with the pretty little wolf. And more anxious to defend her. He started to cut in.

She slashed him a glance, a clear "back off" in her eyes.

He hesitated. If this was a wolf thing, his interfering could harm her pack standing.

Fine, he'd back off—for now. He stepped to the side, a hand cocked near his waist. Not for a gun, but ready to plunge under the sweater vest for the row of charged magical talismans that studded his belt.

"I don't like your attitude, missy. We're going." Bruiser grabbed Emma and hauled her toward the door.

She dug in her heels. "*No.*"

The wolfman slapped her face, so hard it left a red mark on her creamy cheek.

Gabriel forgot all his talismans, took one step, and planted a fist in the wolfman's snout. *Bam.*

Bruiser rocked back on his heels. His hand sprang open, releasing Emma.

Shocked gasps from the employees gave way to a quiet cheer or two.

Mentally, Gabriel facepalmed. He was a crunchy-even-in-milk *idiot*. Yeah, that punch felt satisfying, but it as good as announced that he'd had a raging hard-on for sweet, soft Emma for two months. A freeze potion or calm amulet would've worked more subtly.

Bruiser straightened, rubbing his snout. "Why you...you *fucker...*"

Gabriel shifted his weight to the balls of his feet. This could get ugly.

"You heard Dr. Light." Another male dressed in Choice Buy blue, equally tall with Gabriel, glided up to stand beside him. "Private party."

Male, not man, his black hair and low, growling bass hinting at his panther heritage. This was Gabriel's familiar, Pan, in his human form. If Gabriel had become a powerful battle mage, it was mainly due to Pan's wisdom and teaching.

Which meant the panther was going to kick his butt later for being so obvious. But in private.

Casually, almost negligently, Pan slid a foot forward into a fighting stance. He pointed toward the exit. "Leave."

One by one, the store employees cinched up behind Pan and Gabriel. Gabriel didn't need to see their expressions to know they were glaring buckets at the wolfman, because the bully paled and fell back a step.

Blustering, "This isn't over," the he-wolf spun and marched out.

Pan rolled his golden eyes.

Gabriel jerked his chin at the wolfman, and Pan, reading him flawlessly, followed.

"Thank you, Dr. Light." Emma appeared in front of Gabriel, her eyes shining up at him. "I could've probably handled him, but your solution was much more elegant."

"It was nothing." His cheeks heated. Elegant? He'd been fury-driven stupid and clumsy.

But at her words, something male inside him puffed its chest and yodeled.

She took a step closer, placing fingertips on his sweater vest. "You're being modest."

The chest-beater started fantasizing, picturing her throwing herself into his arms—and bed—in thanks. His cock rose in anticipation.

Before the fool penis and chest-beater could take over, his phone rang.

Two scoops of damn it.

He'd shunted the store phones to the answering service. Only a few people had his direct line. His thoughts arrowed to his pregnant sister, Sophia. "I need to take this. Excuse me?"

Emma stepped back with a nod and a sigh. His cock sighed and stepped back too.

He tapped the headset he always wore in the store. Most witches had trouble using advanced technology—their connection with the basic quantum uncertainty that was magic interfered with anything electrical—but he'd developed spells to prevent such interference.

After his parents died in a magically triggered plane crash, he'd made it his life's work.

In case it wasn't his sister, he spieled off, "Choice Buy, Techie Titan Gabriel Light speaking. How may I help you?"

"Gabriel, it's Sophia." His sister's voice was low and stressed, almost breathless.

His own breath hitched. "What's wrong? Is it the babies?"

Sophia had married alpha wolf shifter Noah Blackwood in semi-secrecy last month, the forbidden witch/shifter coupling in defiance of the Witches' Council taboo.

At first Gabriel was happy for his sister. Noah was a fine male and loved Sophia to pieces. Then Gabriel's familiar Pan had done a bit of research into the Council laws. Gabriel had already known intermagical cavorting was a felony. Life in prison for a witch caught doing the horizontal tango with a shifter.

But a witch princess having children with an alpha wolf? Death sentence.

Sophia said, "The babies are fine."

He breathed in relief.

"But I'm not. Gabriel, a Council Enforcer is about to jail me, and you're my one phone call. I'm accused of *Coeuntia cum Lupo.*"

Mating with a wolf. Gabriel's worst fears had been realized.

www.ingramcontent.com/pod-product-compliance
Lightning Source LLC
Chambersburg PA
CBHW030335310726
48979CB00001B/34

* 9 7 8 1 9 4 0 9 5 8 2 5 5 *